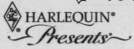

HARLEQUIN®
Presents~

Fantastic Stories for Fall!

Emma Darcy is back with *The Playboy Boss's Chosen Bride,* the story of arrogant Jake Devila and Merlina, who grabs her chance to make him see that she's not just his dowdy, reliable secretary. Penny Jordan is on sizzling form with *Master of Pleasure*: Sasha thought she'd walked away from Gabriel Cabrini, but now he possesses her once more. Julia James guarantees dark desire in *Purchased for Revenge*: Greek tycoon Alexei Constantin has only one thing on his mind—vengeance. If that means bedding Eve he'll do it. Jane Porter delivers drama, glamour and intense emotion when Spanish superstar Wolf Kerrick claims Alexandra, his rags-to-riches bride, in *Hollywood Husband, Contract Wife*. For a touch of regal romance, choose *The Rich Man's Royal Mistress*, the second part of Robyn Donald's trilogy, THE ROYAL HOUSE OF ILLYRIA. Virginal Princess Melissa falls under the spell of man-of-the-world billionaire Hawke Kennedy. In Elizabeth Power's compelling *The Millionaire's Love-Child*, Annie and former boss, Brant Cadman, are reunited in a marriage of convenience when they discover that their babies were swapped at birth. While Anton, the Comte de Valois, demands that Diana become his bride when she becomes pregnant. But what is behind his proposal? Find out in *The French Count's Pregnant Bride* by Catherine Spencer. Bought and bedded by the sheikh—the explosive passion between Prince Malik and Abbie could turn an arranged marriage into one of Eastern delight in Kate Walker's *At the Sheikh's Command.*

Men who can't be tamed...or so they think!

If you love strong, commanding men,
you'll love this miniseries.
Meet the guy who breaks the rules to get
exactly what he wants, because he is...

HARD-EDGED & HANDSOME
He's the man who's impossible to resist...

RICH & RAKISH
He's got everything—and needs nobody...
Until he meets one woman...

He's RUTHLESS!
In his pursuit of passion; in his world
the winner takes all!

Brought to you by your favorite
Harlequin Presents® authors!

Jane Porter

HOLLYWOOD HUSBAND, CONTRACT WIFE

HARLEQUIN®

TORONTO • NEW YORK • LONDON
AMSTERDAM • PARIS • SYDNEY • HAMBURG
STOCKHOLM • ATHENS • TOKYO • MILAN • MADRID
PRAGUE • WARSAW • BUDAPEST • AUCKLAND

ISBN-13: 978-0-373-12574-6
ISBN-10:   0-373-12574-7

HOLLYWOOD HUSBAND, CONTRACT WIFE

First North American Publication 2006.

www.eHarlequin.com

Printed in U.S.A.

All about the author...
Jane Porter

Born in Visalia, California, I'm a small-town girl at heart. As a little girl I spent hours on my bed, staring out the window, dreaming of far-off places, fearless knights and happy-ever-after endings. In my imagination I was never the geeky bookworm with the thick Coke-bottle glasses, but a princess, a magical fairy, a Joan-of-Arc crusader.

My parents fed my imagination by taking our family to Europe for a year when I was thirteen. The year away changed me and overseas I discovered a huge and wonderful world with different cultures and customs. I loved everything about Europe, but felt especially passionate about Italy and those gorgeous Italian men (no wonder my very first Harlequin Presents hero was Italian).

I confess, after that incredible year in Europe, the travel bug bit, and I spent much of my school years abroad, studying in South Africa, Japan and Ireland.

After my years of traveling and studying I had to settle down and earn a living. With my bachelor degree from UCLA in American studies, a program that combines American literature and American history, I've worked in sales and marketing, as well as being a director of a non-profit foundation. Later I earned my master's in writing from the University of San Francisco and taught junior and high school English.

I now live in rugged Seattle, Washington, with my two young sons. I never mind a rainy day, either, because that's when I sit at my desk and write stories about faraway places, fascinating people and, most importantly of all, love.

Jane loves to hear from her readers. You can write to her at P.O. Box 524, Bellevue, WA 98009, USA.

With love for my sister, Kathy Porter.

PROLOGUE

THE WEDDING WAS NOT supposed to happen.

This was a charade, a job she'd been hired to do. But the charade was supposed to have ended long before they ever went to the altar.

Long, Alexandra Shanahan silently repeated, clenching her bouquet of lilies, blue hydrangeas, white orchids and violet freesias tighter between stiff clammy hands.

This was all such a horrible mistake she couldn't even concentrate on the minister's words.

My God, she didn't even *like* Wolf Kerrick. Even four weeks of being squired around Hollywood as his newest love interest hadn't endeared the man to her.

In fact, four weeks of playing his girlfriend had only made her dislike him more. He was horrible in every sense of the word.

He was too rich, too successful, too powerful. He was too much of everything, and that alone made her uncomfortable, but the fact that he didn't respect women infuriated her. He treated women like playthings, taking what he wanted, when he wanted, and discarding without remorse when inexplicably bored.

And now she was his wife.

Alexandra swallowed, stunned, silenced, undone.

She, who could handle anything, she who never wavered in the face of danger, she who took risks and loved challenge, welcoming adversity with open arms, was now married to the world's most famous film star.

Spots danced before Alexandra's eyes and she gulped in air, trying to clear the fog from her head. If she didn't know herself better, she'd think she was going to faint.

She couldn't faint.

It was too much of a photo opportunity.

She must have inhaled too sharply, because suddenly Wolf's hand was at her elbow.

"You better not faint," he growled in his rough accented English, a sexy combination of Irish and Spanish vowels that left women weak at the knees. But that was Wolf's magic.

He was the quintessential bad boy, times a thousand, and everybody's celluloid dream.

Six feet three and impossibly broad through the shoulder while lean in the hip. He looked as good naked in love scenes as he did in a tuxedo shooting the latest James Bond thriller.

Alex's jaw jutted and she tugged her arm from Wolf's touch. "I won't," she whispered defiantly, even though she wasn't sure she wouldn't faint. Truth be known, she was scared, scared in a way she hadn't been since first moving to Los Angeles four years ago.

It'd been a long four years, too.

Four years of struggle, attempting to crawl up the ladder of Hollywood fame. And now she was here. Sort of.

Wolf's grip on her arm tightened. "Then smile. You look as though you're dying."

"If only I were so lucky." Then she forced another tight smile just in case any of the guests could see her face. This was her wedding, after all.

"I'm your dream man. Remember?"

Those had been her words, too, her exact words, but they'd been uttered in a moment of panic, at the height of a crisis. She would have never claimed him otherwise.

Alex's stomach rose, threatening to embarrass her right then and there. Oh, God. What had she done?

Biting her lower lip, Alexandra battled the second wave of nausea even as the Santa Barbara breeze lifted her veil, sending the lace and her long, artfully styled curls blowing around her face. Married to Wolf Kerrick. Mrs. Wolf Kerrick.

Alexandra Kerrick.

Her eyes squeezed closed, her hand shook where it rested on Wolf's arm.

Why had she thought she could play his girlfriend?

How could she have ever thought she'd be able to manage him?

And why had she come to Hollywood in the first place?

CHAPTER ONE

Beverly Hills, California
Five weeks earlier...

ALEXANDRA SHANAHAN had thought being invited to lunch with Hollywood's most powerful actor was too good to be true.

She was right.

"You want me to *what?*" Alexandra Shanahan asked incredulously, staring at Wolf Kerrick as though he'd lost his mind.

"Play my new love interest," he repeated, his deep voice nearly flat.

Wolf Kerrick's love interest. How ludicrous. Beyond ludicrous.

Wolf Kerrick...and her? Alexandra would have laughed if her stomach wasn't doing wild cartwheels.

Everything, she thought woozily, about the lunch was wrong. The impossible-to-secure reservations at the famous Beverly Hills Hotel's terrace restaurant. The bright blue sky overhead. The dizzying fragrance of the terrace garden's roses and gardenias.

When she'd first sat down at the table, she'd introduced herself—silly, but since they'd never officially met, it'd seemed like the right thing to do.

Wolf had repeated her name thoughtfully. "Shanahan. Sounds familiar."

"There's a famous football coach by the same name," she'd answered nervously, trying to ignore the excited whispers of the other restaurant patrons. Everyone had been watching them. Or at least watching Wolf. But then, he was a megastar and sinfully good-looking, so she couldn't really blame them.

"Maybe that's it," he'd answered, leaning back in his chair. "Or maybe it's familiar because it's Irish."

She'd managed a tight smile before dropping her gaze, already overwhelmed by his formidable size and presence.

Wolf Kerrick was bigger, broader, stronger, more male than nearly any other actor in the business. There was no mistaking him for any other actor, either, not with his Spanish-Irish black hair, dark eyes and sinful, sensual mouth.

"Daniel said you had a job offer for me," she'd said nervously, jumping straight to the point. There was no reason to stall. She'd never be able to eat in his company, so ordering lunch was out of the question. Best just get the whole interview over and done with.

"I do."

She'd nodded to fill the silence. She'd hoped he'd maybe elaborate, but he hadn't. Her cheeks had scalded. Her face had felt so hot even her ears had burned. "Daniel said he thought I'd be perfect for the job."

Wolf's dark head had tipped, his black lashes dropping as he'd considered her. After an endless silence he'd nodded once. "You are."

She wasn't sure if she should be flattered or terrified. He seemed so much friendlier on the big screen, more approachable in film than he was here in flesh. Right now he was anything but mortal, human. Instead he was like a dark warrior, an avenger with a secret—and dangerous—agenda.

"I'm looking to fill a position," he said flatly.

"Yes," she echoed, hands knotting together in her lap.

"The role of my new love interest."

She nearly tumbled from her chair. *"What?"*

She stared at him so hard his face blurred.

"It's a publicity stunt," Wolf said in the same flat, almost bored tone. "The position would last approximately four to six weeks. Of course, you'd be well compensated."

Shocked, mortified, Alexandra felt as though she'd burst into flames any moment. "But I—I…couldn't," she sputtered, reaching for her water glass even as a rivulet of perspiration slid down inside her gray linen jacket. She was broiling here on the terrace. She'd dressed far too warmly for lunch outside, and with the bright California sun beating down on her head she thought she'd melt any moment. "I don't date—" she broke off, swallowed convulsively "—actors."

Wolf's jaw shifted. A trace of amusement touched his features. "You don't have to. You just have to pretend to date me."

Him. Wolf Kerrick. International film star. Spanish-Irish heartthrob. Alexandra gulped more water. She was so hot she could barely think clearly. If only she'd dressed more appropriately. If only she'd thought to bring someone to the meeting with her. Her boss, Daniel deVoors, one of the industry's top directors, had sent her here today, telling her Wolf Kerrick had a proposition for her. She'd thought maybe Mr. Kerrick needed a personal assistant. It hadn't crossed her mind he'd be interviewing for a lover.

"Why?" she whispered.

"You're young, wholesome, ordinary, someone the public could relate to."

Young, wholesome and ordinary, Alexandra silently repeated, feeling her heart jump to lodge firmly in her throat. He didn't find her attractive even though she'd made such efforts today. Alexandra rarely wore makeup, but today she'd used a little mascara and a touch of lipstick, and obviously it'd made no difference. She was still wholesome and ordinary. She took a deep breath, suppressed the sting of his words. "But I still don't understand…."

"It's a PR move aimed at damage control." Wolf shifted in his seat so that his powerful body seemed to dwarf the table and the terrace and the day itself.

Alexandra's brows furrowed. She was finding it increasingly difficult to keep focused on what he was saying, disappointment washing through her in gigantic waves. She'd been so thrilled to meet Wolf Kerrick, to have this chance to interview with him. Last night she'd barely slept. Today she'd woken extra early and showered and dressed with such care....

But now...now she just felt hurt. Disappointed.

There was no job, just this ridiculous proposal.

Her temper stirred and she sat taller. "Damage control?" she repeated, trying to keep up with him. "Why would you need damage control...?" Her voice faded as it hit her, in one lucid swoop. *Joy Hughes.*

This was about Wolf's affair with Joy Hughes.

And looking across the table, it all came together. Mr. Kerrick didn't want to hire a love interest. He didn't want to be meeting her or sitting here in public having this conversation. He was doing this—speaking to her, asking her to play a part— to help repair his damaged reputation, and she knew who and what had damaged his reputation. His year-long affair with the very married film actress, Joy Hughes.

"Does this have to do with your...*affair?*" she asked awkwardly, torn between anger and shame that Daniel deVoors would even suggest her to Mr. Kerrick as a possible love interest.

Wolf Kerrick's lips suddenly pulled back in an almost wolflike snarl. "There was no affair."

Alexandra's heart jumped, but she didn't cower. "If there was no affair," she said huskily, fingers balling into fists, "you wouldn't need me, would you?"

Wolf leaned forward, dark eyes flashing, jaw jutting with anger. "There *was* no affair."

His dark eyes held hers, fierce, penetrating, and the stillness following his words was as dangerous as his tone of voice.

She felt the blister of his anger, as well as his underlying scorn. Yet she was angry, too. He must think she was stupid or naive to take everything he said at face value. And she might be naive, but she wasn't stupid. Alexandra met his gaze squarely. "Everyone knows you and Joy have been involved for the last year."

Wolf and Joy Hughes were both megastars. Bigger than film stars, larger than life, they personified Hollywood power and glamour. So much so that when they'd secretly linked up earlier in the year, their affair—Joy was still married to another Hollywood heavyweight—made headline news and had remained there for nearly six months.

Even now she remembered how their photos had been on every cover of every weekly tabloid—for months. "It's not exactly a secret," she added.

The planes of Wolf's face hardened, his high cheekbones growing more prominent. "The media fabricated the relationship. I thought the interest would die. I told Joy as much. It didn't."

He paused, considered his words. "The public's fickle. Today they're enthralled by rumors and gossip, tomorrow they're appalled. But the stories have gotten out of hand. The bad press will soon influence the box-office takings. I can't take that chance, not when it'll hurt every single person who works on my films."

He was right about that much, she agreed, biting her lower lip. She'd been in Hollywood four years, had worked for Paradise Pictures for nearly three and knew that a low-grossing film impacted everyone. A low-grossing film left an ugly black mark on everyone's résumé.

Rubbing at a tiny knot of tension throbbing in her temple, she tried to see her part in this. "But to generate new press by pretending to have a relationship with me? It's such an old Hollywood trick. I didn't think it was done anymore."

His long black lashes lifted and his dark gaze searched hers, his scrutiny so intense it left her feeling strangely exposed. "The studio wants proof that Joy and I aren't an item. Being seen with you would be the proof they need."

"Just by being seen with me?"

"That's how the tabloids work. They snap their photos, run their stories and publicly speculate about celebrities' happiness and future, often without interviewing one reliable source." His tone was rueful, his expression mocking. "After one week of being together in public, we'll be an item."

"That's all it takes?"

"Sometimes only one photo is necessary." His mouth

slanted. "But I should warn you, the pressure will be intense. The paparazzi are everywhere, photographers camp outside my door. Once reporters learn your name, they'll hunt down information on you—where you work, what you do, who you've dated—" He broke off, looked at her from beneath arched brows. "Do you have any scandals in your past, anything the press can dredge up?"

Stunned to silence, she shook her head.

"Old boyfriends with an axe to grind?" he persisted.

Again she shook her head. She'd hardly ever dated. Growing up on an isolated ranch, there hadn't been many chances to date, and moving to Los Angeles at nineteen had nipped her desire to date in the bud. The men she'd met in Los Angeles were often shallow, materialistic and crass, nothing like the men she'd been raised with, none revealing any of the male qualities she admired, like strength, courage, confidence, generosity.

Men in Los Angeles loved cars, tans and expensive restaurants. Oh, and women with fake breasts.

"There's nothing in my past worthy of tabloid interest," she said, briefly thinking of her mom who'd died when she was young and her oldest brother's wife who'd been killed in a car accident. But those weren't the kinds of things the gossip magazines would be interested in. Those were the personal heartbreaks that lay buried between the covers of photo albums, baby books and high school graduation diplomas.

But those personal heartbreaks were also one of the reasons she'd left Montana. Having grown up in the shadow of five older brothers, Alexandra needed space. Independence. She needed to be her own person and have control over her life.

Playing Wolf Kerrick's new love interest would strip her identity as well as her control.

She'd be followed, photographed, harassed.

"I'll make it worth your while," Wolf said quietly, as if able to read her mind, or the emotions flickering over her face. "I've met with Daniel and your studio. They're willing to offer you a significant promotion if you take the position. And when the assignment ends, you'll be offered an A.D. position with Daniel."

"Assistant director?" she repeated under her breath, dazed by the idea of really being involved in making pictures and not just taking coffee orders.

"Yes."

For the first time since Wolf had presented her with the proposal, she was tempted to accept, she really was. To escape from photocopy hell and actually do something on a film...to leave the office behind and go on location...to be involved with real decision making versus how much liquid sugar was needed to properly sweeten the lighting technician's double-shot iced coffee...

But looking at Wolf, she knew her decision wasn't quite so simple. Wolf was a man. An actor. A very popular actor as famous for his skills in the bedroom as his talent on-screen.

And maybe Wolf was notorious for bedding lots of women, but she couldn't do that—wouldn't do that. It's not who she was.

But what if Wolf expected that?

She shot an uncertain glance up into his face. "Mr. Kerrick, I think you should know right now, up front, that I don't do the casting-couch routine." Her heart raced as she considered his hard features, his firm, sensual mouth. "I won't do it. It's not how I was raised."

His lips curled up, a flicker of wry amusement touched his dark eyes before just as swiftly disappearing. "I've never needed to convince or pressure a woman into bed."

"Yes, I know," she said, pulse still pounding like mad. "But I wouldn't want you to think that later I'll do things—"

"Miss Shanahan, rest assured that there's no risk of that. Forgive my bluntness, but you're not my type."

Her face flooded with heat even as her blood turned to ice. Oh, God. How humiliating. But she'd practically asked for that, hadn't she?

Painfully embarrassed, Alexandra felt her insides curdle and cramp. Of course she wasn't his type. Of course he wouldn't want to take someone like her to bed. He could have any woman in the world, why would he want to be with her?

"I'm sorry," she said, voice noticeably husky, "but I don't

think this is going to work. I'm not who or what you need." She fumbled for her purse, finally finding it at her feet, next to her chair. "And I'm not about to try to change to please you or anyone else."

She rose to escape, but Wolf reached out, caught her hand, kept her from fleeing.

"That's where you're wrong." His deep voice, pitched low, vibrated inside her as his dark eyes, a glittering onyx, held her transfixed. "You're exactly what I want and need."

His words shook her, but it was his touch, that scalding press of skin on skin, that made her knees buckle. With his hand around her wrist, she felt electric, charged, different. "I know I'm no beauty queen, but there's no reason for you to be cruel—"

His fingers tightened around her wrist. "Cruel? I'm paying you a compliment. I've picked you to play the role of my lover." His voice deepened, betraying his Dublin roots. "I wouldn't ask just anyone—"

"And I'm to be flattered by that?"

"*Yes.*"

She tugged at her hand, hating the ruthless edge in his voice, that raw, hard, male quality that made him want to dominate her and everything else in his world. "That's where you're mistaken." Tears shimmered in her eyes. "Because I'm not flattered and I don't take it as a compliment that you've chosen me to fill a role in your life. I'm not an accessory, Mr. Kerrick. Not for you, not for anyone!"

She stole a quick breath, noticed the diners around them watching in rabid interest. "People are staring," she said softly, a faint catch in her voice. "Please release me and let me go."

"I'll release you, but I want you to sit down and finish this—"

"It *is* finished," she flashed furiously.

"No, it's not. Sit down. Now." He exhaled. "Please."

Alex slowly sank into her chair again, her purse falling limply to her lap.

Wolf leaned forward, his dark eyes never leaving hers. "Don't let your pride get in the way, Miss Shanahan. Your boss told me you're smart, ambitious. This is an opportunity to make a name for yourself."

Her nausea had returned, stronger than before. "Make a name for myself as what? Your fake girlfriend?" She stared at him incredulously. "You think I should jump at your proposal, be flattered because I'm a plain-Jane girl and don't get out much, is that it? And yes, I'm ambitious, but unfortunately not ambitious enough to date you. Not ambitious enough to pretend to be your girlfriend to get a promotion. I find it digusting that I'd gain industry status—respect—simply by being seen around town with you. That's not the way life should work—"

"Maybe it's not the way it should, but it's the way it does."

"And doesn't that strike you as immoral? Wrong?"

"No. It's practical."

"Of course it would seem so to you. You're the man that dates married women!" And with a violent jerk, she broke free and rose to rush from the table.

Fighting tears, Alexandra squeezed through the tables lining the terrace, wound her way down a pink painted hallway to the ladies' room even as his words rang in her head.

Perfect for the job. Damage control. Publicity stunt. Pretend to date me. Practical.

The tears fell even before she'd managed to lock herself inside the bathroom stall.

This was exactly why her father hadn't wanted her to come to California.

This was exactly what her brothers had predicted would happen.

They'd all said she was too young, too inexperienced to survive in a dog-eat-dog city like Los Angeles, and she'd been so determined to prove them wrong. So determined to make it on her own and do it right.

But playing Wolf Kerrick's girlfriend would be far from right.

The tears trickled down her face, and she scrubbed them away with a furious fist.

He'd pay her to be seen with him.

He'd make sure she was compensated.

Alexandra's throat squeezed closed. She felt as though she were gasping for air on the inside, fighting for calm and control.

And then it hit her. She didn't have to go back to the table. She didn't have to see Mr. Kerrick again or endure any more of his painful proposal.

She could just go. She could just leave and get her car and return to work.

It was as easy as that.

Calmer now, Alexandra exited the stall, rinsed off her face, patted her damp face and hands dry. The valet attendant had her car key. She had her purse with her. She'd just go now.

Alex left the bathroom but had only taken two steps when she froze, her body stiffening with horror.

Wolf Kerrick was waiting for her. And standing, he was even taller than she remembered.

She felt all her nerves tense, tighten. Even her heartbeat seemed to slow. "The men's restroom is on the other side," she said lowly.

"I know."

"The bar is the other direction—"

"You know I'm waiting for you."

Alexandra drew a quick, shallow breath. She was exhausted. Emotionally flattened. All her excitement, all her good feelings about meeting Wolf Kerrick were long gone. "There's no point. There's nothing more for either of us to say—"

"There's plenty. You can say yes."

My God, he was arrogant and insensitive. "I don't *want* to say yes."

"Why not?"

She flinched at his curt tone. It was clear he was used to getting his way and didn't like being thwarted. "I'd never sell myself—"

"This isn't slavery. I'm offering you a salary."

"And I want to make it in Hollywood my way."

"And what is your way?" he taunted. "Making copies? Answering phones? Getting coffee?"

Alexandra's cheeks flamed. "At least I have my self-respect!"

"You might respect yourself even more if you had a job that actually challenged you."

"My goodness but you're insufferable. You should fire your managers, Mr. Kerrick. They've got you believing your own PR, and that's a huge mistake."

He shocked her by bursting out laughing, eyes creasing with humor. "You really don't like me, Miss Shanahan, do you?"

"No."

"Why not?"

"It doesn't matter."

"It does to me."

"Why?" she retorted fiercely, spinning to face him, hands balled at her sides. "Does everyone have to be a fan? Do you want everyone lining up for your autograph?"

Still smiling, his dark eyes raked her. "No."

"Because I'd be lying if I said I liked you. Maybe once admired you, lined up to see your movies, but that was before I met you. Now I see who you really are and I don't like you or your chauvinistic, condescending attitude."

He jammed his hands into his trouser pockets, rocked back on his heels. "Your honesty's surprisingly refreshing."

"Were you ever nice?"

His lips pursed, black brows pulling as he mulled over her question. Reluctantly he shook his head. "No." Then the corner of his mouth tugged into a sardonic smile. "But you don't have to like me to date me."

"That's revolting."

"Alexandra, if you're not an actress and you don't date actors and you can't get yourself promoted out of the copy room at Paradise Pictures, why stay here in Hollywood? Why not just pack your bags and go home?"

She felt a pang inside her, the muscles around her heart tightening. She'd asked herself the very same question many times. "Because I still want to make pictures," she said softly. "I hope to one day be more involved, hope I can somehow make a difference."

He studied her a long moment, his expression closed, eyes

hooded. "You can make a difference," he said finally. "You can help make a picture—and save the jobs of dozens of people. We're to start filming *The Burning Shore* in a little over a month's time. Work with me. Let's get the film into production."

Alexandra bit down, pinched her lip between her teeth. She'd love to make a difference, do something positive, learn something new. She'd love to be challenged, too, but she didn't trust Wolf. "You think we could generate positive press together?"

He'd never looked so somber. "If I didn't, I wouldn't be here now."

CHAPTER TWO

WOLF ACCOMPANIED Alexandra to the front of the hotel, where she'd left her car with the valet attendant.

Lush purple bougainvillea covered the hotel's pink stucco entrance, and the fragrant blossoms of potted lemon and orange trees perfumed the air, but Wolf gave his surroundings scant attention.

Alexandra could feel the weight of Wolf's inspection as they waited for her car to appear.

The problem wasn't only the offer. And the issue wasn't just her morals or her values. It was her lack of experience.

She didn't know how to manage a man like Wolf Kerrick and couldn't imagine how one would even date a man like him.

But they won't be real dates, she reasoned. *They're pretend dates. It's not as if you'll really have to kiss him or touch him or be physically involved.*

Heat washed through her at the very idea of getting physically close. She really did need more experience. "If you gave me some time," she said after a moment, "allowed me a chance to think about your offer properly, I might say yes." She looked up, met his gaze before quickly looking away. "But I don't want to be pressured."

She drew another deep breath, flexed her fingers to ease her tension. "And if I did agree, how would this work?"

If he felt any elation or sensed that he'd won, none of it showed on his face. "We'd draw up a contract, include a enerous financial compensation, as it's probable you'll miss ome workdays due to events and premieres, and then begin going places together to be seen."

He made it sound so simple, she thought, and yet she wasn't a glamour girl, the sort to be invited to fancy parties or industry premieres. No, she was the girl raised by her dad, grandpa and ive older brothers. There hadn't been a woman in the house, ot since her mom died when Alexandra was five. Growing up, he was the original tomboy.

"And what makes you think people will believe you…and …are together?" she asked, pushing thoughts of Montana and he Lazy L ranch from her mind. "I'm not your…usual choice n dates."

"Lots of stars date makeup artists, casting directors, the like."

She hesitated. "Some actors do, but not you."

"You can't believe everything you read in the tabloids."

Maybe, she thought, and maybe not, but she'd seen the pictures of the women he dated. He liked starlets and models, opless dancers and magazine centerfolds, his taste typically unning toward women with more cleavage than brains. And Alex didn't even have to look down at her not-so-impressive hest to know her strength was not in her cup size.

Years ago, back in junior high school, she'd learned that here were only two avenues open for women: the one for retty girls and the one for smart girls. Even in high school it ad been one or the other—cheerleaders and beauty queens or ookworms and future librarians. Girls certainly couldn't be oth. And since Alexandra knew she wasn't pom-pom-girl retty, she'd decided then and there to be smart. Damn smart. We both know I'm not pretty enough to be taken seriously as our new love interest."

"You could be if you tried to do something with yourself," Wolf nswered with brutal candor. "Alexandra, you don't even try."

She bit down, not knowing where to look. "I don't try ecause I know already what I am and who I am. And I don't eed makeup or fake hair or nails or a tan to make me something I'm not."

"Which is what?" he asked quietly.

"A bimbo. I'm not going to be a bimbo. I want to be respected. Taken seriously. And if I change myself—"

"You're changing your hairstyle, not your soul."

Her head jerked up.

"You're smart," he added. "Serious. And I'm sorry, but that eliminates the bimbo category for you."

She should have been flattered. Instead his words merely left her even more flustered.

Every time he looked at her she felt sparks on the inside, little bits of hot fire flaring here and there. It was like being a human sparkler, only worse because the heat didn't die.

"I just don't want to be laughed at," she said after a moment. "People can be unkind. I know the tabloids are famous for publishing unflattering photos and pointing out celebrities' flaws."

"Before we go public, you'll meet with stylists, receive wardrobe consultation. I have a team of professionals who will help ease you into the transition."

Alexandra was intrigued despite herself. "When would that happen?"

"As soon as you signed the contract."

Alexandra tried to imagine being groomed by top Hollywood stylists but couldn't. She might have lost twenty pounds since moving from Montana to California, but she still thought of herself as the sturdy country girl who'd worn cowboy boots before high heels. "A beautiful starlet would be far easier to introduce to the public," she said in a small voice.

"I'm not interested in squiring around a young actress desperate to make a name for herself—"

"But in real life—"

"This is real life, and I'm quite aware that I'm responsible for dozens of people's jobs. I just want to get *The Burning Shore* made and I want to do it without emotional complications."

She fell silent, digesting this. "You don't want anyone to fall in love with you."

His dark eyes creased, his mouth compressed. "That's exactly what I'm saying."

Thankfully her practical little blue Ford Escort appeared that moment in the famous hotel drive.

The uniformed valet climbed from the driver's seat and held the door for her.

Wolf walked her to the car. Alexandra slid behind the steering wheel. "I'll call you," she said.

"You've my number?"

She stared up into his dark eyes, seeing the hard, beautiful lines of his face, and her panic grew. No one had a face like Wolf. No one had his charisma either.

It'd be suicide to do this, she thought, absolute disaster—if not for him, then for her. She wasn't as sophisticated as he was, nor did she have his experience.

"I still have the card Daniel gave me. He wrote your cell number on the back."

Smiling faintly, Wolf closed her door and stepped away from the car. "Take your time, think about your options and call me when you're ready."

She hesitated and then leaned through the open window. "You think I'm going to say yes, don't you?"

His faint smile grew. "I know you will."

"Why?"

"Because you're a smart girl and you'll soon realize this is the opportunity of a lifetime."

The opportunity of a lifetime, she repeated over and over driving home, her hands shaking on the steering wheel and her insides doing nonstop flips.

The opportunity of a lifetime, she repeated yet again as she parked her car in the tiny garage adjacent to her California bungalow, one of the tiny nondescript row houses built in Culver City during the forties and fifties.

Her house was small, and until recently she'd shared it with another girl. But since the girl had a job transfer to Boston, Alexandra was now covering the rent by herself and it was tight. She'd considered getting another housemate but was so enjoying having the space all to herself that she hadn't gotten anybody yet.

And if she did sign the contract to play Wolf's new love interest, she wouldn't have to get a roommate, she'd be able to pay the entire rent herself.

Alexandra loved the thought of that.

Since moving to Los Angeles she'd really struggled, both financially and emotionally.

She'd taken a job waitressing and then a part-time job temping for an independent film studio, answering phones, handling mail, playing general office errand girl, which was mainly going to Starbucks and getting everyone's favorite espresso and latte.

Alex discovered that she liked being useful in the office. She was good in the office—quick, smart, agile, she could multitask and never needed to be told anything twice.

After a year working for the independent film company, she answered a Paradise Pictures ad she saw in *Variety* and was hired to assist intense, brainy directors and producers with whatever needed to be done.

She'd worked for Paradise for nearly three years now and she thought she'd proven herself on more than one occasion, but the promotion had never come.

Why?

It wasn't as though she couldn't handle more responsibility. She actually needed the risk, craved change.

In the kitchen, Alexandra took out the business card Daniel had given her several days ago, the one with Wolf's private number. She tapped it on the counter, flipped it over to the personal cell number scribbled on the back and tried to imagine the next four weeks.

New clothes. Input from a stylist. Exciting parties.

Smiling nervously, she bit her lip. It'd be scary but also fun.

Then she thought of Wolf Kerrick and the whole concept of fun went out the window, leaving her unsure of herself all over again.

But it's an opportunity, she reminded herself sternly, *and that's what you want.*

Quickly she picked up the phone, dialed Wolf's number.

"It's Alexandra Shanahan," she said when he answered, dispensing with any preamble. "And I'll do it. But before anything else happens, I want the offer—and the studio's promise about the assistant director position—in writing."

"Of course."

She held the phone tighter. "And working on B-rate flicks doesn't count. I want to work on major studio films. Big-budget films."

"Certainly."

She folded one arm over her chest and pressed a knuckled fist to her rib cage. "I want to be clear that this is a job, and I'll treat it like a job. I'll do what I have to for the cameras, but I won't do anything inappropriate."

"And what is inappropriate?"

"Kissing, touching, sex."

"There's got to be a certain amount of intimacy for the camera."

"Only for the camera, then, okay?"

"Okay."

"I mean it, Mr. Kerrick."

"I've got it all down, Miss Shanahan. You'll get the contract tonight. It should be there by seven."

The contract did arrive at seven. But a courier service didn't deliver it. Instead Wolf Kerrick brought it himself.

She hadn't expected Wolf and she'd answered the door in her faded blue sweatpants, cropped yellow T-shirt and bare feet in dire need of a pedicure. Without her contacts, and in her glasses, with her hair in a messy knotted ponytail on top of her head, Alex knew she looked more like a librarian than the sex symbol required.

"Hi," she said awkwardly, tugging on her ponytail, trying to at least get her hair down even if she couldn't make the glasses vanish.

"Cleaning house, are you?" he asked.

"I didn't expect you."

"Mmm. But maybe I should come in. Two photographers tailed me. Red car on the right and the white car that hopped the curb. They're taking photos of both of us as we speak."

Alexandra opened the door so Wolf could enter.

As Wolf glanced around the house, she peeked out the living room curtain, and just as Wolf had said, the red car and the white car were out there, and both drivers held cameras with enormous telephoto lenses. "Those are some huge camera lenses," she said.

"I learned the hard way that you'll want to keep your curtains closed. Otherwise they'll get shots of you walking around."

She dropped the lace panel and faced him. "How did they know you were coming here?"

"There is always someone tailing me. Has been for years." He dropped onto her beige couch, extended his denim-clad legs so they rested on her oak coffee table and looked up at her with piercing dark eyes. "How long have you lived here?"

"Almost three years." The abruptness of his question was less disconcerting than the fact that Wolf Kerrick was stretched out in her living room, looking very relaxed-and comfortable—in a loose gray T-shirt, with his thick black hair tumbling across his forehead. "Why do you ask?"

"There's not much furniture."

"My former roommate took it all with her to Boston," she answered, thinking that even dressed down in jeans and a T-shirt, Wolf looked like a film star. It was his bone structure, coloring, the easy way he carried himself. He was more than beautiful, he was elegant and intense and physical. Sexy.

Alexandra exhaled in a painful rush.

That was really the problem. He was far too sexy for her and had been from the time she first laid eyes on him—which was in a movie, of course—eight years ago. In *Age of Valor,* just his second film, he'd played a soldier. And while he wasn't the lead in the film, his performance was so strong, he stole the show. Alexandra remembered sobbing when his character died in the film, dramatically blown to bits just before the movie's end. She'd liked him—the man, the actor, the character—so much she couldn't bear for the story to end without him still in it.

She had been fifteen at the time, just starting her sophomore year of high school, and of course she had known it was just a movie and he was just an actor, but she'd never forgotten his face or his name.

Wolf Kerrick.

Amused by the girl she'd once been, Alexandra took a seat

on the edge of the coffee table across from him. "Shall I sign the contract?"

Wolf's dark head tipped and his long black lashes dropped, brushing his high, strong cheekbones. "Think you can do this?"

Growing up, she'd been the ultimate tomboy. As the baby of the Shanahan clan, she'd stomped and swaggered around in her cowboy boots. But moving to Southern California had killed her confidence, and she was only just starting to realize how much she missed her old swagger.

She'd once been so brave, so full of bravado.

How had moving to California changed her so much? Was it Hollywood? The movie industry? What had made her feel so small, so insignificant, so less than?

"Yes. I know I can," she said forcibly, and strangely enough, she meant it. She was the girl who'd roped calves and ridden broncs and jumped off the barn roof just because her brothers said she couldn't. She was the girl who didn't take no for an answer. If she could ride a bull, she could date a wolf.

Alexandra's lips curved at her own feeble joke, but her smile faded as Wolf's black eyes met hers.

"Think you can handle me?" he murmured.

Her heart stuttered. She knew what he was asking. Like everyone else who read the tabloids, she knew he'd been arrested more than once for fighting and heard it didn't take much to bring out the street fighter in him.

She also knew that women found him irresistible, and having once been one of those giddy girls who threw themselves at him, knew she'd never behave so recklessly again.

"Yes," she answered equally firmly, ignoring the cold lash of adrenaline. "You won't be a problem. You might be a famous actor, but you're also just a man. Now give me the contract and let's get this over with."

He handed her the contract and a pen, and Alex spread the document on the table to read while she tapped the pen against her teeth. The form read correctly, all the terms were there, everything she asked for given.

With a confident flourish, Alexandra scrawled her name at

the space indicated. "There," she said, lifting her pen and handing the paper back to him. "Signed, sealed, delivered."

"My little lovebird," he mocked, taking the paper and folding it up.

Her cheeks heated. Her blue eyes locked with his. Her heart was pounding wildly, but she held his gaze, kept her chin up, refusing to show further weakness. "I won't be broken, Mr. Kerrick."

"Is that a challenge, Miss Shanahan?"

"No. I'm just stating a fact. I had some time to think about your offer, to look at the pros and cons, and I've agreed to do this not because it helps you but because it helps me. I know now what I want and I know what I need to do to get there. And you won't keep me from succeeding. There's too much at stake." And then she swallowed hard. "For both of us."

He studied her from across the table, his forearms resting against his knees, his eyebrows black slashes above bold dark eyes. "There will be pressure."

She rose to her feet. "I anticipate it."

"The attention will feel intrusive at times."

"I've considered that possibility, as well."

"You're truly prepared to take this all the way? Ready for the makeover, the new hair, the wardrobe and revamped image?"

"Yes."

He stood. "Tomorrow you'll pay a visit to the Juan Carlos Salon in Beverly Hills. The salon is expecting you. It'll be a long day. The car will be here at seven."

"I don't want a limo, Mr. Kerrick."

"It's part of the role, Miss Shanahan. And now that we've agreed to this little play, it's time we dropped the formalities. We're lovers now." He slowly moved toward her. "You're Alexandra and I'm Wolf and we're a very happy new couple."

He was standing so close to her now she could hardly breathe. "Right."

"Just follow my lead," he said.

"Your lead," she whispered, feeling the warmth of his body, his strength tangible and real. She tipped her head back, looked up into his face, with the strong cheekbones and high forehead, the piercing dark eyes.

"I'll make it easy for you."

"You're that good an actor?"

"I'm that good a lover."

She took an involuntary step backward. "You said there'd be no sex—"

"In public, it's my job to seduce you. To make the photographers sit up, take notice."

She inhaled hard, thinking he was the devil in the flesh. "In public, yes."

He leaned down and brushed the briefest kiss across her flushed cheek. "But in private, we're just friends, remember?"

She felt her stomach fall and her breath catch as his lips touched her cheek. The whisper of his warm breath sent fingers of fire racing through her veins.

Wolf headed for the door. "Don't forget to set your alarm clock. The limo will be here early."

Alexandra leaned against the door after Wolf closed it.

Her heart was still pounding and her tummy felt coiled in a new and aching tension.

This was not going to be easy. Pretending to be Wolf's girlfriend would be the hardest thing she'd ever done.

And then she pulled herself together. *No more negative thoughts,* she told herself. *No more running scared.* She'd signed the contract. She had to go for it now.

And she would go for it.

She'd been in Los Angeles four years and she was hungry. Really hungry. Hungry like one living on the streets, digging out of trash cans, looking for something to fill you up, get you by.

Because, God knew, she wanted to go somewhere. She was determined to go all the way, too, all the way up, to the top. Fame, fortune, power. She wanted the whole bit.

It was time to do what she'd left Bozeman, Montana, to do. Time to make Hollywood hers.

CHAPTER THREE

THEY WERE CUTTING HER hair off.

The next morning, covered in plastic drapes, Alexandra stared aghast as Juan Carlos lifted chunks of her waist-length hair and began to chop it off to shoulder length.

She'd had long hair—really long, down to her butt—since she was a little girl. Being the only daughter, her father had wanted her to be a princess and insisted she leave her hair long. Soon he'd learned her hair was the only thing he could control, as his princess preferred jeans, boots and playing with LEGO, blocks and army trucks.

Alexandra had kept her hair long for her dad and now she found herself fighting tears as it was whacked off.

"It'll be beautiful. You'll be beautiful," Juan Carlos reassured, catching sight of her tear-filmed eyes in his station's mirror. "Be patient. You'll see."

Alexandra wanted to believe him. And it was just hair, nothing more important than that. And if she couldn't handle getting her hair cut, how would she handle the other changes coming in the next few weeks?

With her long hair in pieces all over the floor, Juan Carlos patted her shoulders. "Now we change the color."

Thirty minutes later, Alexandra was still trying to get used to the smell of bleach and chemicals from the cream applied to her hair. They were doing a two-color process—overall color and highlights—and the smelly foils on her head made her want to gag. Did some women willingly do this?

Juan Carlos had told her he was giving her warm amber highlights and promised to make her a Hollywood golden girl.

Alex wasn't so sure about the golden part.

Squeezing her eyes shut, she battled her nerves, drew a deep breath and counted to ten.

At ten, she opened her eyes, caught a glimpse of her silver-wrapped alienlike self in the mirror and closed her eyes again.

This was not going to work.

Back at home five hours later, Alexandra looked in the mirror at the new, improved version of her. Her hair shimmered with a multitude of highlights, precision-cut to fall in thick, sexy waves around her face, playing up her black-lashed blue eyes and the strong cheekbones she didn't know she had.

The makeup artist had shown her how to use color and liner to subtly darken and define her lips, her brows, her eyes.

And studying the new, improved Alexandra, she thought she looked good. *Pretty*. Pretty in a way she'd never been before. Feminine but smart. And confident. Strong. And that's the thing she hadn't known she could be on the outside. On the inside, she liked to roughhouse with the best of them, riding bareback, helping in the roundups, slinging barbwire along with the ranch hands. She'd learned early that she had to keep up with her brothers or she'd be left behind, relegated to the kitchen and the laundry room at home, and if there was anything Alex didn't want, it was woman's work. Housework. Domestic chores that kept her locked inside when the sky was huge and blue beyond the windows of the house, where the land stretched endlessly, waiting for exploration and hours of adventure.

Alex's lips half curved, and she stared, fascinated, at the face of a woman she realized she barely knew.

She really was pretty, almost pretty like the girls in magazines. And maybe it was makeup and expensive hair color and a professional blow-dry, but she wasn't the fat girl she'd been at eleven and twelve and fifteen. She wasn't even the sturdy, healthy nineteen-year-old who'd arrived in Hollywood eager to make movies.

Reaching up, she touched the mirror, touching her reflection, the shimmering tawny lips, the dusty glow of cheeks and eyes that looked midnight-blue in the bathroom lights.

"Be confident," she whispered. "Be brave."

And with one last small, uncertain smile, she turned away from the mirror and left the bathroom, hitting the light switch on her way out.

In the living room she turned on the front porch light, and before she could decide if she should turn on the stereo or the TV or pick up a magazine to read, the doorbell rang.

Butterflies danced through her middle, spinning up and into her head.

God, she was nervous. Scared.

Why was she so scared? It wasn't as though she'd never been out with Wolf before. It's not as if she hadn't ever been alone with him either.

Hands pressed to her sides, she took a deep breath and reminded herself of all the reasons why she'd come to L.A. and all the things she wanted to learn, to do, to prove. Maybe Wolf Kerrick was way out of her league and maybe this was going to be a rocky couple of weeks, but doing this, playing this part, would help her succeed.

Wiping her damp hands on the side of her black trousers, she moved to the door and opened it.

And then he was there, even bigger than she remembered, taller, more intimidating. And twice as beautiful.

Maybe that's the part she found so disconcerting, too. Because she'd been around big men all her life. Brock was six-four, and Cormac a half an inch below that. But her brothers were more rugged—handsome but lacking the dark Latin sensuality that made Wolf's eyes just a little too dark and his lower lip a little too full and his black lashes a little too long. It'd be one thing if he didn't know his effect on women, but he did, and it only made him more dangerous. Wolf wasn't so much charming as lethal.

"I just need to get my purse," she said, opening the door wider and doing her best to hide her nerves. "Do you want to come in?"

"If you're just getting your handbag, I can wait here."

She silently disappeared, legs distinctly trembly as she went to the couch to scoop up the little evening bag she'd laid out earlier. The bag was so pretty, a small, black, handsome couture bag that looked simple but cost a fortune. Alexandra had seen the price tag when the stylist had presented it and gasped. The stylist had merely winked. "It's covered in your budget," she'd said.

Now Alexandra clutched the bag beneath her elbow, feeling briefly like a glamorous celebrity herself. She knew it was all hair and makeup and wardrobe, but still, it was such a treat, such a delight to feel genuinely pretty for a change.

"So what are we doing tonight?" she asked, returning to join Wolf at the door.

"Thought we'd have some drinks, get a bite to eat."

Alexandra nodded and closed the door behind her. She turned to head down the front steps, but Wolf hesitated and, reaching behind her, checked the door, giving the knob a twist, making sure it was locked.

She shot him a quick glance as they walked toward his Lamborghini. The fact that he'd double-check her door touched her, made her feel surprisingly safe.

She was still looking at him when his head turned and his dark eyes met hers. She shivered inwardly and amended her last thought. Make that as safe as one could feel with a wolf.

It was a warm night and the fog hadn't yet moved in. Wolf headed to Santa Monica, where he pulled in front of the luxurious Hotel Casa del Mar, which stood next door to its famous sister property, Shutters on the Beach.

The Casa Del Mar, built in 1926, was once the grandest of the opulent Santa Monica beach clubs and hotels, and a recent fifty-million-dollar renovation had returned the historic property to its former magnificence.

Although she'd never been there until tonight, Alexandra knew that the Veranda, the elegant lobby lounge, was famous for its literary crowd. Screenwriters and novelists hung out in the celebrated bar, with its enormous windows overlooking the sea and the plush velvet chaises and chairs scattered for comfortable seating.

The Veranda was packed when they entered, but miraculously an alcove opened up for Wolf and the cocktail waitress immediately took their drink orders.

Alexandra had thought the lounge was crowded when they walked in, buzzing with laughter and conversation, but the buzz seemed even louder now that Wolf had entered the room.

Everyone was looking their way, men and women alike watching Wolf, openly fascinated.

"I forgot. You're such a star," Alexandra said, sitting on the edge of her red velvet chair, afraid to relax and possibly ruin her artfully styled hair or carefully applied makeup.

"You forgot?"

"Well, I forgot it was like this." She pressed her hands against the chair's edge. "Everyone always looks at you. They watch everything you say and do. It's incredible. I guess that's what *star* means. You're the focus of everyone and everything."

He shrugged, unconcerned. "People are curious. They want to know if I'm as interesting as the characters I play."

"Are you?"

He laughed softly. "No." Reaching out, he took her hand, brought it to his lips. He kissed her fingertips and then curled her fingers over his and kissed the back of her hand, all while his gaze held her transfixed. "I'm sorry to say, I'm really quite boring."

She didn't believe him, not for a second.

Not when his eyes, glowing with an inner fire, belied his words, and Alexandra felt her belly clench as his lips moved across her skin.

He was not boring. Not now. Not ever.

Wolf tugged her hand, pulling her up and out of her chair, drawing her firmly toward him.

"Wolf," she whispered in protest.

He ignored her, pulling her down into his chair so that she sat awkwardly on his lap.

"*Wolf,*" she repeated fiercely, blood surging into her face, darkening her cheeks.

"You were too far away," he said.

She felt the hard heat of his lap through her thin black

trousers and it threw her, flustered her so that she tensed, going rigid in his arms. "And now I'm a little too close," she choked, her breath catching in her throat as his hand moved to the small of her back, holding her more securely.

"I think you're perfect."

"I feel ridiculous."

"Have I told you how much I like your hair?"

She felt as though everyone in the Veranda lounge must be looking at her. "Please let me off. People will talk."

"But isn't that the point? Don't we want them to?"

He was right, of course, but even knowing why she was on his lap didn't change the way she felt or how her body was responding—because it *was* responding. Her nerves were jumping and strange things were happening inside her, sharp hot streaks of sensation starting with the tight coil in her tummy and then racing to her breasts as well as lower, deeper, making her legs twitch and her mind wander.

"Stay here for our drink and then I'll let you off," he said, rubbing the small of her back as though it were perfectly ordinary for her to be on his lap with his strong hands casually caressing her, and maybe he could pretend ease, but Alexandra felt as though she'd pop out of her skin any moment.

His touch wasn't soothing and she wasn't relaxing. She couldn't relax, not when he was stirring dormant feelings and even more dormant nerve endings.

Her lower back was tingling, sizzling with heat and pressure, warming to life beneath the dizzying touch of his hand, and that burn was starting to make her ache in places she didn't want to ache. Her breasts were already growing fuller, more sensitive, and her belly was coiling hot and tight, making her think of escape. Relief.

She looked up into his face.

Had he had this effect on her four years ago? Somehow she didn't think so. She couldn't imagine it. Would she have very different feelings about him today if he had? "I think that's long enough," she whispered.

"Not even close." And then his hands were on her waist,

fingers sliding up toward her breasts, and she sucked in air, eyes widening in mute fascination.

He was turning her on. Really turning her on—and in public, too.

"*Wolf.* Let me go. Now."

"We're supposed to be lovers."

Her mouth was parched, her lips painfully dry, and she licked her lips, trying to moisten them. "I know, but does this have to be in public?"

"If it's not public, no one will know."

Alexandra thought she'd run to the bar and make her own drink if the cocktail waitress didn't return soon. "But maybe…maybe we can be one of those mysterious couples that don't really *do* PDAs."

"PDAs?" he asked, his head tipping back against the velvet chair as he watched her with lazy interest.

His hair was thick, glossy black, and he wore it a little long. And in a way it reminded her of a wolf pelt—thick, dense, male.

And Wolf was very male.

Alexandra struggled to swallow. She couldn't remember ever being this thirsty before. Her body was burning and her throat felt absolutely parched. She pressed her lips together, feeling her teeth beneath.

"PDAs?" he prompted again.

"Public displays of affection."

The corner of his mouth lifted. "But I've no problem with public displays of affection if I like my woman."

He'd trapped her in his eyes, and she gazed helplessly into the deep brown depths, a color somewhere between cocoa and black coffee, thinking they seemed endless, so dark, so deep, so alive with that unique fire of his.

One of his hands trailed up her spine, tracing her backbone and the little vertebrae between.

She shivered beneath the light caress, aroused despite her fierce desire not to be.

He had exactly the right touch, not too firm, not too delicate. And there was something about him, about his size and strength, about the tilt of his head and the mocking glint in his eyes that made her feel small and pretty and feminine. But not just feminine. Desirable. As though she were the only one in the room. The only woman in Los Angeles. California. Make that the planet.

Her pulse quickened and she found herself staring into his dark eyes, eyes that from far away were black but close like this had the smallest splinters of silver. Those shards of silver made her wonder if it was the lounge's soft light or the fire that burned within him that made his eyes glow, turning him into some fierce and beautiful work of art.

Fire and ice.

The words whispered through her head and wrapped uncomfortably tight around her heart.

Because that was really who he was, she realized, looking at his face, the hard but expressive sensual features, the glossy black hair, the equally strong black brows.

"Now you're staring," he teased, his hand sliding higher up her back to rub between her shoulder blades, finding the little knots and balls of fear and tension. And magically he smoothed the knots away, rubbing firmer and then lighter, heating her, melting that resistance within her.

She wasn't sure when she began to lean into him, seeking his touch, his warmth, but somehow his chest was where she wanted to be.

The cocktail waitress materialized with their drinks, and Wolf gestured for her to set them on the low table at his elbow. Smiling, she left the drinks and moved on, but not before giving Alexandra a brief inspection from beneath her lowered lashes.

Alexandra saw the look the waitress had given her and she wondered if everyone would look at her that way.

Wolf handed her martini glass to her before lifting his. They clinked glasses and Alexandra tilted her chocolate martini to her mouth, curious about a drink she'd heard of but never tried.

It was smooth, hot, strong, sweet, and she wrinkled her nose as she swallowed.

"Don't like it?" Wolf asked, watching her.

"It's different."

"I take it different is bad."

She smiled ruefully. "Different can be good. But in this case, different is just different."

"Mmm." His dark eyes glowed, and she felt, if not saw, the laughter within.

"You're not laughing at me, are you?"

"Actually I am."

And as she opened her mouth to protest, he caught the back of her head in his hand and pulled her close to cover her lips with his.

She inhaled at the sudden touch of his mouth on hers. It was a shock to her senses, his mouth so cool and firm, tasting of sweet chocolate and icy vodka. She shivered, her breasts peaking. At her shiver, his mouth hardened, the kiss deepening, the pressure parting her lips.

Her head spun, her senses swam, her body danced with pleasure that was as hot and sweet as it was electric.

The electric part dazzled her all over again, and blindly she leaned into him, searching for him, searching for more of the sensation and pleasure he offered.

Finally he lifted his head. She blinked, tried to focus, but she could only feel her mouth, soft, swollen, sensitive and it amazed her, this way he had of winning her over, taking her objections and melting them as surely as he'd just melted her.

Lifting her fingers to her mouth, Alex pressed down on her lips, feeling how the lower lip quivered and how her blood raced in her veins liquid-hot.

One kiss and she wanted more.

One kiss and she wanted to slide her hands into his thick ebony hair, twine her fingers through the glossy strands and hold tight, hold his face to hers so she could feel him, his beard and mouth, jaw and chin.

"You're looking a little more relaxed," he said, catching her hand in his and bringing it to his mouth, where he kissed the pulse beating frantically in her wrist.

"I think it's the chocolate martini," she said unsteadily.

His eyes creased. "I thought it was my kiss."

She lifted her glass to her mouth and took a greedy gulp to hide the fact that he was making her nervous all over again. Those butterflies in her stomach had returned, only this time they felt more like forks of jagged lightning.

The chocolate-flavored martini slid down her throat, cool and tantalizing but also empowering. The cocktail made her feel stronger, calmer than she would have otherwise.

By the time they headed for home, close to midnight, Alexandra was laughing and surprisingly at ease.

She didn't know if it was that first chocolate martini or Wolf making an effort to be charming, but she'd ended up having fun.

After drinks at the Casa Del Mar they'd driven to Houston's for steaks and salads and glasses of wine. Again everyone had stared when they'd entered the darkened brick building, and again the hostess had magically found them a table.

Wolf hadn't been the only celebrity dining at Houston's that night, though. There'd been several other well-known entertainers, and two of them, both men, had stopped by their table to say hello.

Now Wolf was walking her to her door. After she unlocked the door, she stepped inside, and he followed her in, closing the door behind him. For a moment she felt a spike in nerves again, nerves and anticipation. Would he kiss her again?

But instead of a kiss, he checked each room, made sure everything was as it should be before saying good-night, giving her a platonic peck on the forehead and returning to his car.

His brotherly kiss jolted her back to reality. The kiss on the forehead was a kiss in private, a kiss behind closed doors and an indication of how things really were.

She wasn't his love, wasn't his girlfriend. She wasn't even really his date. She was just a girl hired to play a part. Any kisses, any whispers, any sexy innuendos were for the public and the press, wherever the hidden photographers might be.

Alex leaned against the door and remembered the kisses

earlier. There'd been so much heat between them. When he'd kissed her, she'd felt unbelievable. Glamorous. Funny. Delicious.

"Delicious," Alex repeated, turning out the small hall light and heading for her bathroom, where she pulled her hair into a ponytail and washed her face, getting rid of the makeup.

In bed, Alex curled onto her side, covers pulled up high, so high that they covered her chin and the middle of her ear.

So you learned something important tonight, she told herself. *You learned that there's a difference between real and pretend, truth and fiction. Tonight was make-believe. And it's okay to enjoy the make-believe, but don't get it confused with reality.*

You're doing a job. That's it.

No emotions, no hopes, no feelings.

This, she reminded herself sternly, is business.

The next morning Alex was at work when the flowers arrived. Three dozen very long-stemmed pink roses in a stunning hand-blown glass vase. Oohing and aahing, the entire Paradise Pictures office staff broke away from their tasks to look over Alexandra's shoulder as she read the card.

Thank you for an unforgettable night. Looking forward to another. Wolf

Kristie, one of the other production assistants, snatched the card from Alexandra's hands. "Wolf?" she said, flashing the card at everyone. "There's only one Wolf I know of."

"Hmm," was all Alexandra said as she sat down in her chair and pushed the extravagant roses toward a corner of her desk to make some room to collate the scripts she'd just photocopied. It was one of the first jobs she did every morning. There were always script changes during the night, and the new, updated scenes had to be distributed to the cast and crew immediately.

But Kristie wasn't to be put off. She leaned across Alexandra's desk and held the small white florist card in front of Alexandra's eyes. "Wolf."

Alexandra looked up, her gaze meeting Kristie's. "I think that's what it does say."

"Wolf Kerrick?"

Alexandra suppressed a sigh. "What do you want me to say, Kristie?"

The young, bubbly production assistant from Duluth, Minnesota, arched her eyebrows. "You're seeing Wolf Kerrick?"

Alexandra shrugged as she reached for the next set of pages and stapled the corner. "I don't know if I'm seeing him. We went out last night. Had dinner and drinks—"

"Is that the first time?"

"Um, well, not exactly. We've had lunch. And then he's stopped by my house a couple times—"

"For real?"

Alexandra suppressed a smile. Kristie's expression was priceless. "We've only just met in the past week. Who knows where it'll go?"

But Kristie wasn't looking at the card anymore, she was studying Alexandra. "It's more than that. Something's going on. You're different, you know. You're…pretty."

Alexandra's eyebrows lifted. "I wasn't pretty before?"

"Not like this."

Rolling her eyes, Alexandra grabbed the florist card from Kristie and shoved it in her desk drawer. She tried to focus on the job in front of her, but Kristie hadn't budged and the other girls were still watching and waiting.

She knew she had to say something. They were desperate for a morsel of news, some juicy little tidbit, and isn't this what Alexandra had agreed to do? Play the part? Become Wolf's new love interest?

Shaking her head, Alexandra finally looked up. "If he proposes, I'll let you all know."

Three o'clock that afternoon, the studio's main number rang and the receptionist took the call and then buzzed Alexandra to let her know she had an incoming call from Wolf Kerrick. Unfortunately the receptionist chose to use the intercom to tell Alexandra of her call, instead of a private line.

With Kristie and the other girls staring in rabid fascination,

Alexandra picked up her phone and took the call off hold. "Alexandra Shanahan," she said as crisply as possible.

"Wolf Kerrick," the voice answered at the other end of the line. His voice was deep and husky and tinged with amusement.

Alexandra didn't know if it was the timbre of his voice, or the amusement in it, but it immediately set her teeth on edge. "Hello."

"Can I bring the coffee girl a coffee?"

Aware that Kristie was inching forward, Alexandra ducked her head, trying to avoid being overheard. "No, thank you."

"How about I take you for a coffee?"

"Wolf, I'm *working*."

"Not very hard."

"What does that mean?"

"It seems to me you're just sitting there, staring at your desk."

"How do you know?" Alexandra demanded before noticing the office had gone strangely silent. Lifting her head, she saw that Wolf, dressed in loose dark denims and a black linen shirt unbuttoned halfway down his chest, had entered the front doors and stood next to the receptionist's desk talking on his cell phone.

My God, he looked gorgeous. And sinful. "What are you doing?" she whispered urgently into the phone, trying to duck her head so he couldn't see her face or the telltale blush turning her cheeks a crimson pink.

"Watching you."

She squeezed her eyes shut. "Why?"

"Because I want to."

"Wolf."

"Can you just do that with a little more passion in your voice?"

"No!" Alexandra started to slam the phone down and then, remembering she had an audience, hung the receiver up more gently. Phone down, she watched Wolf slowly saunter toward her through the rows of desks.

She heard the girls whispering excitedly as he passed. Wolf had to have heard the whispers, too.

Reaching her desk, he stood over her, his linen shirt half open, giving her and everyone else a glimpse of burnished bronze skin and hard, toned muscles. His dark eyes half smiled down at her, and yet there was nothing sleepy about him. He had the silent, watchful air of a wolf before it attacked.

"I'm stealing you away," he said.

Alexandra hadn't expected to see Wolf for days. She'd thought maybe by the weekend he'd call her, contact her, set something up for the future, and yet here he was, at her desk, causing trouble.

And she wasn't ready for trouble. Didn't think she'd be ready for his kind of trouble for a long time. Last night had taken something out of her. Last night had been a tease, a torment. She'd had so much fun with him that she'd imagined he'd been enjoying her company just as much. Instead he'd been acting.

Acting.

Alexandra smiled her brightest, most confident smile to cover her trepidation. "I wish I could go. But I've so much work. I've a million things to do and Daniel—"

"Has already given you permission to take off early." Wolf smiled down at her, but the smile didn't quite reach his eyes. "So get your purse and let's go."

CHAPTER FOUR

IT WAS A GORGEOUS afternoon, hot, sunny, the sky a dazzling California blue. Wolf was driving a different car than he had last night, a gleaming red Ferrari that looked brand-new.

A studio head, just leaving his office and heading for his car, noticed the Ferrari, too, and wandered over to shake Wolf's hand and compliment him on the car.

"That's a Superamerica, isn't it?" he said to Wolf as he shook his hand. "Hardtop convertible."

Wolf opened the passenger-side door for Alexandra. "It is."

"I was reading about the car's revolving roof recently. Doesn't it open up in ten seconds?"

Wolf was heading to the driver's side now. "It does."

"What are they? Half mil?" he asked as Wolf settled behind the wheel.

Wolf put the key in the ignition, started the engine. "A little less than that," he said before putting the car into reverse.

The other man whistled. "Beautiful car."

Wolf nodded agreement and drove away. But Alexandra sat next to him, dumbfounded.

"This car is worth half a million dollars?"

Wolf shot her an amused glance. "It's not that much. It's closer to a third of a million. But I can see you don't approve."

She studied the car's interior. The steering wheel wasn't exactly normal. It had paddle shifters on the wheel, but other than that it looked like an ordinary—albeit very clean—sports car. "I don't understand why anyone would spend so much money on a car."

"I have the money."

"Yes, but—"

He was leaving Culver City behind and heading for Santa Monica. "But what?"

"But you could do a lot of good with that money. You could feed starving children and build houses for the homeless and things like that." She stopped talking, bit her lip, stared at her hands, inspecting the spa manicure she'd gotten at the salon yesterday. "I know it's none of my business. I just wish I had the means to help more people. I think we should all help more people."

Wolf looked at her for a long, silent moment. "I agree," he said quietly before returning his attention to the road.

They traveled in silence down Santa Monica Boulevard and then north on Highway 1 wrapping the coast toward Pacific Palisades and scenic, craggy Malibu.

Wolf drove well, fast but confidently, and with the cliffs to the right and the sea to the left, Alexandra felt as though she were part of a movie or some reality television show.

He had been unusually quiet since she made her comment about helping others, but she wasn't sorry for thinking people should help others and she wasn't sorry for thinking an expensive car like this was a waste of money. He could buy whatever he wanted and she could think whatever she wanted. They weren't really a couple. They didn't have to agree.

Finally Alexandra couldn't take the silence any longer. She made a pitiful stab at conversation by asking him, "Are you excited about the new film?"

"Excited?" Wolf repeated, his upper lip curling. "I wouldn't say I'm excited, but I will be glad to work again. Working distracts me. Keeps my mind off other things."

It wasn't the answer she'd expected. She'd imagined he enjoyed acting, thought he would have found a certain fizz factor from being one of the most highly acclaimed actors in the business. "What things?"

His eyebrow arched as he glanced at her. "We all have ghosts and demons."

"And you won't tell me yours."

"No."

Alexandra didn't know if it was his expression or the caustic curve of his sensual mouth, but she felt the strangest flutter inside her middle as though she were nothing but naked nerve endings.

"Do you ever go home?" she asked suddenly, not sure where the question came from but curious about him, curious about his past as well as those ghosts and demons he'd just mentioned.

He shot her a long, assessing glance from beneath his lashes. He knew what she was doing, too. "Ireland or Spain?"

"Which is home?"

"Both, I suppose. I'm bilingual and was raised in both countries."

"Your mother was Spanish."

"From Cadiz," he answered, slowing for the traffic light looming ahead. "I was born in Cadiz, but when I was twelve my parents divorced and I moved with my father to Dublin. Spain is home in ways Ireland could never be, but I'm comfortable in Ireland, I like the people."

"And yet now you're here, in America."

"It's what the career dictated."

Alexandra stole a glance at him from beneath her lashes. "Do you ever regret becoming an actor?"

He hesitated before answering, shifting gears down and then, after the light changed, accelerating until he pulled into the parking lot for the Malibu Coffeehouse.

Turning off the engine, he turned to look at her. "Every day," he said grimly.

After getting their coffee, Wolf drove to one of the scenic turnouts on Highway 1 and parked. Climbing from the car, they moved to the cliff's edge to savor the view.

Wolf drew a deep breath, breathing in the stinging salty air off the Pacific Ocean. He loved the ocean, loved the cliffs of Malibu and Pacific Palisades. This area reminded him of

Ireland's southern and western coasts, especially when the soupy fog rolled in, covering everything in a misty, mournful gray.

If it weren't for the ocean, Wolf didn't think he would have survived so many years in Southern California. He hated L.A. He hated the falseness, the superficiality, the attitude and airs. People in his business—like so many people in Los Angeles—were afraid to be real, human.

They were afraid of their bodies, their age, their flaws, their frailties. Women here went to ridiculous lengths to be beautiful: nipping, tucking, tightening, enlarging, enhancing, sucking, smoothing. They worked on themselves endlessly, refusing to age naturally, fixated on how they looked, how others perceived them, how attractive they were in comparison to other women.

God, he missed real women. He missed wit and banter, laughter and smiles that made the eyes crinkle and foreheads wrinkle instead of ghastly BOTOX-frozen faces. He'd love to share a drink with a girl who could tell a proper story, eat a bag of chips and not immediately worry about her thighs. Sometimes Dublin seemed too far away, and in those moments he missed his old life—the ordinary life before he'd become a celebrity—more than he could say.

Alexandra watched Wolf sip his coffee as they leaned against his half-a-million-dollar car. She felt wrong leaning against a car that cost so much, but he did it so she supposed it was okay for her to do it.

Ever since they'd left the Malibu Coffeehouse Wolf had been quiet, and his expression was unusually pensive now. Always enigmatic, he seemed even more distant than usual. Again she wondered why he didn't enjoy being an actor and why his success—and the accompanying fame—didn't mean more to him.

Was he really so spoiled? Was it arrogance that made him fail to appreciate his achievements? Or was it something else?

"There's nothing planned after this, is there?" she asked, wind blowing, tousling her hair. She tried tucking strands behind her ears, but they wouldn't stay there.

"We've a dinner tonight at Spago."

Any other time Alexandra would have been excited about the idea of eating at Spago. Wolfgang Puck's name and reputation spoke for itself. But she was tired—she hadn't been sleeping well lately—and after the tense afternoon she craved a quiet night at home. Alone. Preferably curled up on her couch with a good book.

"Do I have to go?" she asked in a small voice.

"Yes."

"Why?" she asked in an even smaller voice.

He glanced at her, expression blank. "It's Rye Priven's birthday."

Rye Priven was the newest heartthrob in Hollywood, a gorgeous Australian that had just co-starred in a film with Wolf. The film was in the editing stage now and was supposed to be released at Christmas, when all the big Academy Award contenders were released.

"But Rye Priven doesn't know me—"

"Everyone's coming as a couple," Wolf answered roughly. "You're supposed to be the other half of my couple."

She ducked her head, stared sightlessly at her cup. She was hating being part of the couple right now. Wolf was so intense. And unpredictable.

"Rye's hosting the party himself. He's keeping it low-key," Wolf added. "I think he's only invited six friends, so my absence would be conspicuous, particularly as I already told him I'd be there."

"I'm not saying you shouldn't go," she doggedly replied. "It's just that I don't feel like it."

He looked at her over the rim of his coffee as he took another sip. "You don't like me much, do you?"

"No," she blurted and then winced at her bluntness.

"Why not?" Wolf paused, waited for an answer. "It's a shame you can't be more articulate in naming my faults."

Alexandra shot him a swift assessing glance, but he didn't look the least bit injured. "Your morals and values are deplorable. You could be someone truly great, someone…heroic. But instead you just use people. Take advantage of them. I hate it."

"And you hate me, too."

"I—" she started to protest but then fell silent. She didn't want to start lying to him, because then the lies would never end. It was bad enough she'd agreed to do this, but to become as fake as her role? No. She wouldn't sell out. She couldn't. "*Hate* is a strong word," she conceded. "But I don't like you and I don't respect you. You just seem so bored and spoiled and arrogant. Selfish, too."

"You're a hard woman, Alexandra Shanahan."

She suddenly felt her anger start to melt. She didn't want to be angry, didn't like feeling angry. "You're just used to women falling all over you, desperate to impress you, please you. It's too bad, too, because you'll never know if people like you for you or because you're a famous movie star."

"Or if they like me for my body or my face."

Alexandra nearly choked on her sip of her now lukewarm coffee. "And that's exactly why I don't like you. You're so incredibly…" she drew a rough breath "…so…"

"Yes?"

"Conceited."

"Conceited," he repeated.

"You have so much—you've virtually everything—and you don't even appreciate it."

"And just what is everything?"

She gestured, her hand sweeping up and down. "This. You. Looks, wealth, fame, intelligence, success. You have it all, you have more than anyone else I know. But do you even feel grateful? Do you even have any idea how blessed you are? I don't think so."

"I hired you to play my girlfriend. I'm not paying you to be my conscience."

"I don't think you've even got a conscience!" Alexandra shrugged. "And you're right, none of this is my business. Just like who you pick up and take home isn't my business. Or the number of women you have in a week, that's not my concern either. You're free to take women and use them and abuse them, because as long as they give themselves over to you, you're not doing anything wrong."

"Right."

"Wrong!" Alexandra furiously tossed her cup into the trash bin and spun to face him. "Just because women will let you have them doesn't mean you should take them. Just because women get blinded by your good looks and fame, just because they hope a night of sex will turn into true love, doesn't mean it's okay for you to take advantage of them."

The corner of his mouth lifted. "Maybe I'm not taking advantage of these women. Maybe they're taking advantage of me. Maybe they know one night of sex is just that, one night of sex, and when they leave me in the morning they leave happy to have had one night with me. They've got bragging rights, a chance to talk big—"

"That's horrible."

"To you."

Her hands balled, nails pressing hard against tender skin. "Not just to me but to all women. It's a lack of respect, a lack of awareness of how women think and feel, of how making love makes them think they've fallen in love…"

"You're sounding as though this is pretty personal."

Her chest felt hot and tight, too hot and tight. She felt absolutely undone, beyond her own level of self-control. "Women aren't tissues, to be used and discarded."

"Have I somehow hurt you, Miss Shanahan?"

She turned away, stared out across the busy lights of the boulevard.

Yes.

Yes. Four years ago, you parked your fancy car and we kissed and made out. And then when I fumbled with your damn trousers and belt buckle, you realized I was inexperienced. You realized I didn't know how to touch you or give you pleasure and you got rid of me so fast afterward. If I couldn't give you what you wanted…

Tears filled her eyes and she squeezed her fists against her ribs, pressing hard against her sides, pressing skin to bone. "No," she whispered. "You've done nothing to me."

"Are you sure? Because it's almost as though you've some personal experience—"

"No."

"Good. Then you'll have no objections going to Rye's party tonight?"

Alexandra reached up and swiped away a tear before it could fall. "You still want me to go?"

"Want?" His shoulders lifted. "I don't know if it's want, but you did sign a contract, and regardless of your personal feelings—or even my own—you'll fulfill the contract."

"Even if I hate you," she whispered.

His mouth quirked, eyes dark and granite-hard. "Especially if you hate me. Fewer complications, remember?"

The party that night at Spago was less stressful than she'd feared.

The stylist had dropped off clothes for her to wear—a smart black cocktail dress that was both simple and sexy, very high stiletto heels and a pretty gold charm bracelet that was girlish and fun.

The stylist had shown Alexandra how to pile her hair on top of her head in a messy twist with loose tendrils falling here and there. With small gold studs in her ears and neutral makeup, she looked nothing like the office assistant she was.

Good, she thought, joining Wolf in the car. Because she wasn't going to be an office assistant or production assistant for long. She was going to learn how to direct. She was going to make movies.

Wolf was driving a different car again tonight. This one was a sleek pewter Ferrari from the '60s. Even she could see it was a classic that had been lovingly restored.

"I've seen three cars so far," she said, sliding into the passenger seat. "Are there more?"

Wolf waited for her to buckle her seat belt before driving off. "An entire warehouse full."

"A warehouse?"

"I collect cars." White teeth flashed, and Alexandra couldn't be sure if it was a smile or a snarl. "Something else for you to disapprove of."

Dinner was less tense than the drive to the restaurant. Nearly everyone attending the dinner was a celebrity. She counted four actors, two actresses, a comedian and an R & B singer, along with their respective dates. During dinner Wolf discussed politics with Rye and the R & B singer, and Alexandra was rather surprised by his depth of knowledge regarding world economics and the U.S. trade policy.

"Do I know you?" the man to her left asked when Alexandra turned from Wolf's conversation to her dinner salad.

She recognized the man—an actor named Will Cowell—but they'd never met before. "No," she answered, cutting the apple in her salad.

"Are you sure?"

She stabbed her fork into lettuce, apple, and blue cheese. "Quite sure."

"Hmm." Will studied her, elbow on the table, expression teasing. "Then I *should* know you."

She chewed her salad diligently, hoping he didn't see her blush. Swallowing, Alexandra wiped her mouth with her linen table napkin. "Why is that?"

"Because you don't look like a bimbo—and God knows I need a break from bimbos."

Alexandra laughed. She couldn't help it. "What makes you think I'm not a bimbo?"

"No fake boobs or collagen-plumped lips." He smiled charmingly. "I'm an expert in those things, you see."

Her eyebrows arched, but she took another bite of salad instead of replying. It seemed safer to eat the sweet-tart vinaigrette salad than discuss his expertise in fake breasts and lips.

"Can I have a word with you alone? In private?" Wolf suddenly growled into her ear.

She turned toward him, apple and cheese skewered on her fork. "Why?"

His dark eyes snapped with fire. "Alone," he repeated. "In private."

Wolf stood up, pushed his chair back and took her by the elbow.

With his hand on her lower back, he pressed her through the restaurant and down the hallway until he found a small alcove by the pay phones.

"What are you doing?" Wolf demanded, turning on her. "What game are you playing?"

Alexandra shook her head, nonplussed. "Game? There's no game. I was having dinner, talking to Will—"

"Will's pathological. He has to get in every woman's pants."

She jerked her head back as if slapped. "Well, he's not getting in mine, and we were just exchanging a few words. Pleasantries, that's all."

Wolf's features tightened. "He was looking at you as though he'd devour you any moment."

"If you didn't notice, *I* was devouring my salad."

"You're supposed to be devouring me."

Alexandra gasped with outrage and shock. Her jaw dropped, her eyes grew wide. And then she snapped her jaw closed and came out swinging. "Sorry, Wolf, but I'm afraid I don't have the experience!"

She gave him a shove, her hand connecting with his chest, and she'd pushed at him so hard her wrist did a painful little snap, but he didn't budge.

Wolf felt her hand hit his chest, but he didn't move a muscle. He couldn't. He was wound too tight.

No one and nothing got under his skin, not anymore. He wanted to believe that, but since meeting Alexandra Shanahan, she'd lived under his skin.

His gaze swept her face. "What do you mean that you haven't the experience?"

Her dark blue eyes snapped at him. "I mean that I'm not an actress and I haven't devoured lots of men and I can't do whatever it is you want me to do."

"Are we talking oral sex or intercourse?"

He watched, fascinated, as a wave of color stormed her cheeks.

"And that," she choked out, tendrils of hair falling around her face, "is none of your business."

"Just like my sex life is none of your business."

"That's because you have one and I don't!"

He leaned toward her, trapping her between the pay phone and the wall. "You could."

Another wave of color surged through her cheeks, darker, hotter than before. Her blue eyes shimmered. "It's not in our contract," she said through gritted teeth, nose in the air, cocky as a little girl in a denim skirt and cowboy boots.

"No," he muttered, "but this is." He closed the distance between them with one aggressive step.

Alexandra's heart thumped wildly and she pressed backward, her hands behind her, knuckles tight against the wall. He loomed over her, so tall, so big, so much more powerful, and it wasn't even his height that made him strong or his frame but the force inside him, that fire. He was alive and intense, engaged and aware.

She didn't want him to kiss her, didn't want him anywhere near her. But once his head dipped, it was like last night at Casa Del Mar's Veranda lounge.

Bolts of electricity shot through her, and that was even before his mouth completely covered hers.

And then when his lips did take hers, she felt the electricity again, hotter, brighter, sharper.

He felt good. He felt amazing. Unreal.

Her mouth softened. The pressure of his lips increased and her heart raced, fast, faster, as fire and hunger whipped through her.

She groaned as he parted her mouth with his tongue, groaned again as his tongue flicked the inside of her inner bottom lip, tasting her, teasing her, making her want more of him.

This wasn't a kiss, she realized, dazed. This was his first step in seducing her, taking her, and he intended to do it. Despite the contract.

But would that change when he realized she really was as inexperienced as she said?

Back at the table, Wolf sat with his arm draped over the back of Alexandra's chair. And her chair was close to his—so close that no one could mistake his actions for anything but a sign of possession.

He was claiming her, marking his territory, letting the other men know to stay away and letting other women know he was taken.

Alexandra, he noticed, didn't like it.

"You might as well put a Sold sign on me," she said through gritted teeth.

"That's not a bad idea," he answered, smiling faintly at her pink-cheeked indignation. He'd never met a woman who blushed so much—or made a simple blush so alluring.

Studying her profile, he found it hard to believe she was as inexperienced with men as she claimed. How could she be when she was so ridiculously pretty?

He looked at her thoughtfully, almost clinically, trying to understand what it was about her that made him want to put that Sold sign on her.

Maybe it was that leggy tomboy stride of hers, or her mouth that was endlessly expressive, sometimes set, sometimes pursed, sometimes smiling most beguilingly.

Wolf didn't know which he liked better—that full mouth with the tiny indentation in the bottom lip or the midnight-blue eyes set so wide beneath winged eyebrows.

Or her sharp mind and sassy tongue.

His sardonic smile stretched.

She was a breathtaking combination of girl and woman, funny, sensitive, proud, uncertain. Unlike the women in Los Angeles who pursued him, women who blatantly advertised their interest and availability, Alexandra didn't project her sexuality. It was hidden, secret, and yet when he kissed her, she became a different woman.

She became his woman.

It was as simple as that.

Later, as they drove from Spago back to Alexandra's house,

she sat as far as she could from Wolf in the snug sports car and kept her eyes firmly fixed out the passenger window.

Wolf had reached a whole new level of despicability. He'd shown his true colors, behaved like a member of the animal kingdom more than once.

"You're still upset about the kiss," Wolf said.

His nonchalance only antagonized her further. "Everyone noticed your behavior at dinner." She threw him a disgusted look. "You kept your arm on my shoulder throughout the meal as though you were afraid I'd bolt away any minute."

"I wasn't afraid you'd run away. Your heels are far too high—"

"Wolf, don't play the charming-Irishman card right now, okay?"

"And I like touching you," he continued smoothly as though she'd never interrupted. "You're my girlfriend. It's my prerogative."

"And that's how it felt, too. It was your prerogative to touch me. Your prerogative to kiss me. Your prerogative to do whatever you damn well pleased." She finally turned to face him. "Next time why don't you just pee all over me like an alpha wolf should."

He'd pulled up in front of her house, and turning off the engine, he flashed her a lazy white-toothed grin. "Hmm, kind of kinky for a girl without much experience, but if that's what you want—"

Alexandra threw the door open and jumped out of the car before she had to listen to another word.

And as she undressed for bed, peeling the smart, sexy black dress off, Alexandra wanted to scream with frustration. Spending time with Wolf was hard, far harder than she'd even imagined. It wasn't just one thing, it was everything. He wasn't just physically gorgeous, his personality was huge, his charisma larger than life.

He was far more than she could handle, and she'd known it, she'd known it from the beginning, but she wanted that promotion. She wanted it badly.

And unless you'd been a little girl who'd grown up outside

a small town, you didn't appreciate that for girls in small towns opportunity meant a job at Wal-Mart and success meant one day owning your own car free and clear. Unless you'd been the only girl in a family of overbearing brothers, you didn't understand the value of dreaming, and dreaming big.

Unless you'd listened to the sound of television late into the night, the canned laughter on TV shows and overly loud commercials the only sound in your house after everyone else had gone to bed, you didn't know the definition of *escape*.

You didn't know how important it was to get away and become someone else, something better, something more.

But Alexandra knew all these things, had lived all these things, and she decided years ago she'd have a different life than her mother, her father, her brothers. She'd do it differently than the people who seemed to just get swept along by life.

She wouldn't be swept along. She'd do the sweeping.

She wouldn't ever make anyone take care of her.

But Wolf Kerrick seemed determined to change all that. In fact, if she let herself really think about it, it felt as though Wolf Kerrick was sweeping *her*.

CHAPTER FIVE

ALEXANDRA'S FIRST thought on waking was that she needed to call Wolf immediately, before she lost her nerve.

"We need to talk," she said crisply, her tone no-nonsense when he answered the phone. "You hired me to make things better, not worse, and it's important we find a way to keep our public appearance positive."

If she'd caught him off guard, he gave no indication. "I agree," he said.

Alexandra couldn't read his inflection. "I can't help your image if we can't even communicate," she continued stiffly. "So I propose we work harder at creating clearer communication channels."

"Communication channels, yes."

She understood then that he was, without a doubt, mocking her. And Alexandra knew that she had a choice—she could call him on his attitude, thus detouring from the purpose of her call, or she could let his sarcasm slide. She chose to let his sarcasm slide. "Before we go out again," she persisted, "and before we make another appearance, we need to choreograph the evening."

Wolf cleared his throat. "Are we entering a dance competition, by chance?"

Alexandra chose to ignore this bit of sarcasm, too. "I need to know before we go places what you expect and how we're *both* to behave. I can't wing it anymore. I'm not an actress and I can't improvise the way you can."

There was silence on his end of the phone and the silence seemed to stretch endlessly.

Exasperated, she closed her eyes, counted to five. "Did you hear me?"

"What?" he asked innocently.

"This doesn't have to be difficult," she said through gritted teeth.

"You're right." And then his tone changed, his rough voice deepened. "So let me make this easier. We've a premiere Saturday afternoon. It's a matinee since it's a children's film. I did the voice for one of the characters and I've promised to be there. You'll attend and—" he broke off, hesitated as if searching for the right word "—pretend to enjoy me."

Alexandra flushed hotly. "That's not exactly the choreographed routine I was imagining. It sounds more like a set of military orders."

"But at least you know my expectations."

"And what about mine?" she flashed, furious that she was losing her temper yet again but unable to stop it. He had the most negative effect on her. From the beginning he'd annihilated her self-control.

"Well, you can expect to have your photograph taken, and expect to stand by my side and expect to be paid." He paused. "Is there anything else?"

"No," she choked out, hanging up.

The rest of the week passed too quickly for Alexandra's taste, knowing that on Saturday she'd be with Wolf again, attending the premiere.

She'd only been seeing him a few days, but already she was exhausted, worn out trying to juggle work responsibilities during the day and appearances with him.

Fortunately she was looking forward to the film. Even though it was only a matinee for *The Little Toy Solider,* the newest Pixar animation, Alexandra was looking forward to seeing exactly what happened at premieres.

She'd read about them for years in *People* magazine, seen

the photos of celebrities attending, and now she was finally going to one.

Even better, it was the premiere of an animated film—Alexandra's secret favorite. Back before her brother Brock had been widowed, she used to go into Bozeman, Montana, with his late wife Amy and their kids to see all the Disney films. In her mind, Saturday afternoons were made for movies, and she was glad to be going, eager to see just what kind of cartoon toy soldier Wolf'd be.

A stylist arrived at Alexandra's house early Saturday morning, bringing with her several wardrobe options. Jointly Alexandra and the stylist settled on the low-hipped sexy charcoal trousers cinched by a wide gray croc belt with an enormous round pewter studded buckle. On top she was wearing a burnout velvet tank in a color somewhere between lemon and mustard, topped by a fitted cropped coat of the same rich, saturated color.

She'd accessorized with sleek pewter heels and a chunky two-strand gray-and-white alabaster necklace. Her hair had been flatironed and it hung smooth and sleek past her shoulders. Makeup was even more subtle: pale foundation, lightly lined eyes in gray pencil, lots of mascara and a soft, neutral lip color called Naked for her mouth.

When Wolf arrived at one to pick her up, he was dressed casually elegant in jeans, a white dress shirt and a dark gray Armani jacket. He wasn't behind the wheel today. Instead he had a driver and a limo, important for the red-carpet arrivals.

He was cool and distant during the ride, and Alexandra sat opposite him, savoring the last bit of privacy before they stepped onto the red carpet and into the flash of a hundred camera strobes.

"I almost forgot," Wolf said, reaching into the limousine's side console. He handed her a clear glass tube the size of a rolling pin filled with gold confetti and a single sheet of rolled parchment paper.

She tipped the cylinder to watch gold glitter emerge from the sheer strips of shimmering confetti. "Not another invitation."

"With me, of all people."

She gave him a dark look and tipped the cylinder yet again but at a shallower angle, fascinated by the glitter clinging to the insides of the tube. "So what's this an invitation to?"

"It's for Matt Silverman's fiftieth birthday party."

"Ah." Matt Silverman was the most innovative director and producer in the business today, and everything he did—whether it was a futuristic sci-fi or a historical drama—became a block-buster, guaranteed to garner a half dozen Academy Award nominations, including the coveted Best Picture. "When is it?"

"Thursday." Wolf glanced out the window. Traffic was slow through the 405 and 10 intersection. "It'll be a big party. Black-tie, live band, sit-down dinner in his Bel Air estate's garden. Nearly everyone in the business will be there." He leaned back against the seat, smiled crookedly if not a bit wearily. "But we've got to get through today's premiere and parties first."

She nodded, noticing the shadows under his eyes. "Do you ever get tired of the parties and events?"

The creases deepened at his eyes. His expression turned wry. "All the time."

"But…?"

"Every movie needs publicity, and publicity requires me being out there, doing the interviews, the talk shows, the premieres, the award shows, the parties and fund-raisers."

"And that doesn't even include making the films or the weeks on location," she added.

"You're right, it doesn't."

She'd never really thought about the life of a star like Wolf, imagining that fame, fortune and success made life easier, but she wasn't so sure anymore. "No wonder you're not in love with your career."

He shrugged. "It's a job, and I understand it's a job."

"You don't make it look like a job. You're incredibly talented."

His expression almost gentled. "You don't have to make points with me, Alexandra. I know how you really feel."

She waved her hand, batting away his comment. "If you made one less film a year, that would be less PR, fewer interviews and press junkets and parties, right?"

"One would hope."

"So do that. Make one less film. Or two. Find a way to have more time for yourself. I'm sure there are things you'd like to do."

The corner of his mouth lifted, but his dark eyes were deep, intense. "You're sounding an awful lot like you want to save me. But, love, I can't be saved."

"Yes, you can."

"This isn't a challenge, Alexandra."

She pressed her lips together, held tight to her opinion—and her temper—realizing now wasn't the time to debate him.

Instead she changed topics. "So what would you do if you had more free time? Would you pick up a hobby? Want to travel? Are there places you're anxious to go? What's top of your to-do list."

His eyes narrowed. "Ending world hunger."

Alexandra did a double take. Was he serious? She couldn't be sure, but he wasn't smiling, wasn't making light of his lofty ambition.

"Erasing Third World debt," he continued.

She simply stared at him.

"Stopping the spread of AIDS in Africa." His hard features softened, his expression turning rueful. "Sorry you asked?"

There was something in his face she'd never seen before, something behind the slightly bored, rather cynical mask he usually wore. Something fierce and raw and real. *Real.* For the first time she saw a man, not an actor or star.

Alexandra felt a tug inside her chest, a twinge of muscle that was almost pain. "No."

And then whatever fierce, raw emotion—passion—she'd seen disappeared, replaced by that public mask he wore to keep the world at bay.

With mask firmly in place, Wolf turned, glanced out the window and spotted the crowds lining the sidewalks. "We're here."

The morning after the premiere, Wolf flew to New York for a Monday-morning appearance on *Good Morning America* to promote *The Little Toy Soldier* and then an afternoon taping for the David Letterman show at the Ed Sullivan Theater on Broadway between Fifty-third and Fifty-fourth Streets. If things went well, he hoped to have dinner with friends Tuesday and then return to Los Angeles Wednesday morning.

He'd said maybe they'd have dinner Wednesday night—he'd let her know once he was back in town.

It was odd with Wolf out of town. Alexandra went to work Monday morning thinking she'd feel liberated, but instead she felt rather lost.

Wolf had been taking up so much time—physically and mentally—she didn't quite know what to do with herself now that he was gone for the next three days.

Alexandra tuned in to *Good Morning America* at the studio, caught the tail end of Wolf's interview—he looked so amazing on TV, it wasn't fair at all—and then turned the TV off once the interview ended to get back to work.

Tuesday she wondered if he'd call.

Wednesday she wondered if he'd caught his morning flight and was heading back to L.A.

Instead flowers arrived for her Wednesday noon, four dozen white roses with a stiff white embossed card that read, *Have been held up in NY, will pick you up tomorrow for party. Apologies. Wolf*

Alexandra hid the card before anyone else could see.

He wasn't coming back until tomorrow, until just before the party. And she didn't mind, not really, not until Kristie in the office casually dropped a newspaper on her desk, opened to the Entertainment section with the celebrity gossip column.

The VIP Room

Wolf Kerrick was seen having a cozy dinner Tuesday night with former flame, actress Joy Hughes, at Manhattan's celebrity favorite, Nobu. Are Wolf and Joy back together again?

Alexandra read the gossip item over and over again until her eyes began to burn and a lump formed in her throat. She felt almost…betrayed. Which was stupid since she and Wolf weren't a real couple, but still, they'd been spending so much time together lately that in some ways she did feel as if she was part of Wolf's life. Felt almost like Wolf's woman.

Quickly, before anyone could see, Alexandra wiped away tears, stood up, trashed the paper and went to make her third coffee run of the day.

Wolf picked her up in the limo fifteen minutes after the party officially started, but even then they were among the first arriving at Matt Silverman's fabulous Bel Air estate.

Although it was a private party and media hadn't been invited, dozens of photographers had still set up their cameras on tripods across the street from the Silverman mansion.

Walking through the gardens next to Wolf, Alexandra recognized nearly half the people there. And the other half were probably the really important people—the producers, directors, power agents like Benjamin Foster.

"Did you get my flowers?" Wolf asked as they stopped near the pool to take in the hundreds of floating water lilies illuminated by just as many floating candles.

Alexandra's stomach immediately knotted. "I did."

He turned his head, looked at her. "I'm sorry I was held up—"

"No apologies or explanations required."

She was trying to be poised, but the tartness of her answer gave her pain away.

"You saw the photograph of Joy and me at Nobu," Wolf said.

Had there been a photograph in another paper? Her heart felt strange. Tender. Almost fearful. "No. I just read a little blurb about your dinner in the local paper."

He was still looking at her. "There's nothing between us, Alexandra."

She nearly hung her head and then thought better of it. She was wearing vintage Armani tonight, an exquisite ivory pleated gown that the stylist had brought over yesterday. With the gold-heeled sandals on her feet and the gold band wrapped around her arm she felt beautiful, like an Egyptian priestess or maybe a princess, and she didn't want anything to ruin that.

"It's none of my business," she answered calmly.

"But it is, at least until our contract ends."

She managed a droll smile. "You're too good an actor."

"What does that mean?"

"It means we both know the truth. I'm not the kind of woman you usually date. I'm serious, industrious. I like the quiet evenings in and you—" she broke off and smiled brighter "—are the bad-boy playboy, notorious for all-night parties."

He swore under his breath, a short, sharp, profane curse that caught her by surprise.

Alexandra blinked at him. "I've never heard you curse before."

He took her chin in his hand, lifted it up. "I wish everything was as simple as you make it out to be. I'd love for life to be so black-and-white, but it's not. And you, sweetheart, don't know me." His dark eyes burned into her, promising, punishing. "You know nothing about who I really am, and maybe that's a good thing. Maybe it's better to let you remain sweet, inexperienced, naive."

Alexandra didn't have time to answer or defend herself. People were heading their way, flocking toward Wolf as though he were a beacon of light.

Concealing her chaotic emotions, Alexandra quietly stood next to him. Wolf appeared to have many industry friends. He'd been a Hollywood force for nearly ten years, but it was only in the last two years, since winning the Oscar for *Boys in Belfast,* that he'd become viewed as a serious talent.

Waiters passed glasses of specialty cocktails on gilded wood trays—cocktails like pomegranate martinis and Lemon Drop shooters—and the crowd around Wolf grew louder and more jovial as the drinks were consumed.

Alexandra tried not to wiggle while she stood for the first hour at Wolf's side, but it was difficult not to feel self-conscious given the amount of skin her cream Armani gown exposed.

Fortunately Wolf didn't forget her. Several times in that long hour he broke off his conversation to introduce her, point someone out or try to explain a reference, making sure he included her as much as he could. He even once reached out and touched her upper arm as he talked to yet another woman who'd come to congratulate him on his exceptional performance in his last film.

Two more young women were approaching Wolf now, both stunning, one very fair with straight waist-length blond hair and a figure that looked as though she could model for Victoria's Secret, and the other a sexy, sultry brunette that reminded Alexandra of Wolf's former flame, Joy Hughes.

As it turned out, the blonde *was* a model for Victoria's Secret and she introduced her friend, a former Miss Venezuela who'd come to Los Angeles to pursue an acting career.

Despite Alexandra's presence, the women flirted outrageously with Wolf, touching him, laughing, leaning seductively toward him, showing cleavage Alexandra would never have. But once again Wolf put his hand on her arm, rubbed it as if to reassure her, and some of Alexandra's tension eased. That was until Paige, the Victoria's Secret model, tripped and sent her red pomegranate martini flying—all across Alexandra's exquisite ivory Armani dress.

For a moment Alexandra just stood there, her bare shoulder wet and sticky, her breast and fitted bodice a splash of pale red, with little droplets of red staining the long straight skirt.

A seven-thousand-dollar vintage gown ruined.

She stared at Paige in shock, her gaze riveted to the model's empty glass. Empty because the cocktail was now all over her gown.

For a moment she could think of absolutely nothing to say— at least nothing polite, because on the inside she was livid, fuming. How could a model that pranced down a runway in four-inch heels and enormous white angel wings trip over nothing? And not just spill her drink but dump the entire contents over Alexandra and only Alexandra?

"Are you okay?" Wolf asked, his arm encircling her, bringing her closer to his side.

"I'm fine," she choked out. But she wasn't fine. She was

shaking, trembling in her heels. Her lovely dress was ruined and there would be no easy exit from the party, not with a stain like this.

Wolf flagged down a waiter and requested some soda water and a towel. "Soda water might help," he said.

She nodded, forcing a tight smile. "I'm fine, it's fine," she repeated, but her voice had grown husky. It was humiliating being Wolf's pretend girlfriend, humiliating playing a role and being ignored by everyone and pretending she didn't notice their condescension when Wolf introduced her.

But she understood their snubs, understood why they didn't care to meet her or remember her. Wolf had a reputation for dating and discarding young Hollywood starlets. And being young and reasonably pretty, people probably assumed that Alexandra—Wolf's newest plaything—would soon be gone. These people weren't going to try to impress someone or even be kind to someone who wasn't important.

And she wasn't important. Not to anyone here.

Shame filled her, shame at so many different levels. She shouldn't have signed the contract. Shouldn't have let her own ambition get before her morals. Shouldn't have allowed herself to be used.

Just because she wasn't an actress or a model or someone powerful in Hollywood didn't mean she wasn't valuable.

"I'm sorry." She struggled to maintain her composure. "This is so embarrassing."

"It's not at all." Wolf suddenly looked at Paige and Lulu and gave them such a dark, ferocious look that both women scuttled away. With Paige and Lulu gone, he drew her closer. "And you couldn't embarrass me, so don't say things like that."

Blinking back tears, she glanced up, and the depth of his concern made her see yet again that he did wear a public mask, a coolly amused mask, as though he were always laughing at life. Laughing at himself. But she was just beginning to realize that underneath the mask he wasn't laughing at all. "I should go before the entertainment reporters and photographers spot me looking like this."

She took a deep breath, straightened her shoulders. "Now let me just slip out now so no one can get pictures of us together. You stay here and do what you have to do."

"I'm not going to let you leave alone. If you want to go, we'll go together." Wolf reached inside his tuxedo for his mobile phone. "I'll call for the car."

She covered his hand with hers so he couldn't make the call. "You have to stay. Aren't you making one of the birthday toasts?"

He shrugged. "It's more of a roast than a toast."

"But still, you're wanted here, needed here."

He shook her hand off and punched in the number before putting the phone to his ear. "The speech is already typed up. I could have someone else do it."

The waiter returned at that moment with a small bottle of soda water and two clean white kitchen towels. Wolf hung up, reached into his pocket for a twenty-dollar bill to tip the waiter.

"Thank you, Mr. Kerrick," the waiter said, nodding appreciatively.

Alexandra took the soda water and towels from the waiter. "All right. I'll make you a deal. You stay here, and I'll go find a bathroom and see what I can do to salvage this dress. Okay?"

"Okay."

She nodded and forced a light note into her voice. "I'll be back soon."

Alexandra was heading to the house to look for a bathroom when she crossed paths with Jason Kirkpatrick, a young director she'd met earlier in the year when he'd dropped by Paradise Pictures to discuss directing a film for the studio. In the end, he wasn't hired, but Alexandra had enjoyed her brief conversation with him that morning and she smiled in recognition as he flagged her down.

"Alex! It's Alex, isn't it?" he said, hailing her.

"Yes, although I prefer Alexandra," she corrected. "And it's Jason, right?"

"Good memory." He rocked back on his heels. "So what happened to you?" he asked, lifting her hand that clutched the bottle of soda water to better see the vivid stain ruining her gown.

She'd nearly forgotten the catastrophe and grimaced now. "A famous lingerie model accidentally poured her drink on me."

"That's a lot of accident," he retorted, taking a step into the shrubbery and pulling her with him to let people pass behind them on the curving stone path.

She glanced down at the stain. "I'm thinking the pomegranate martinis are better in the glass."

He laughed. "You're funny."

"Thanks."

His laugh turned to a sympathetic smile. "Why don't you run home and change? The party hasn't even started. It's still only the cocktail hour."

"I'd go home if I could, but I don't want to make Wolf leave—"

"Why should Wolf have to leave? Zip home, change and come right back."

Alexandra's nose wrinkled. "I'd love to, but it's not that easy. I don't have a car and I didn't bring money for a cab. And Wolf—"

"Let me take you." Jason stretched his hands out. "My Porsche is right out front. Wolf's a friend of mine. I'd love to help him out."

"Oh, I don't know if that's a good idea." She glanced over her shoulder, struggling to see if she could find Wolf in the crowd, but the extensive garden was packed. "Wolf might not like it."

"It'll only take a moment and then—snap!—you'll be right back, pretty as a picture." Jason winked. "And trust me, you'll take a better picture in a new gown, if you get what I mean.

CHAPTER SIX

AT MATT SILVERMAN'S Bel Air estate, Wolf walked through the fancifully decorated gardens with the massive jacaranda trees festooned with twinkly lights, searching the clusters of partygoers and guests for Alexandra.

There were so many people—hundreds—that he was forced to look for splashes of cream and white fabric in the crowds to focus his search, and while he spotted several women in light-colored evening gowns, none were Alexandra.

As he headed back through the gardens to the estate's 1930s mansion, Wolf wondered if she had perhaps gone home. Maybe she couldn't get the red stain out of the dress and she hadn't wanted to make a scene.

He frowned as he neared the ornate fountain. Even if she was embarrassed by the stain, he couldn't imagine her just leaving without speaking to him.

And if she had left, how had she gotten home? Had she called a cab? Had a friend picked her up?

Not far from the fountain Wolf spotted his agent grabbing a couple of sushi appetizers from a tray one of the waiters held.

"How's it going?" Benjamin asked Wolf as he popped a bite of sashimi and wasabi into his mouth.

"Good." Wolf's brow furrowed, knowing it wasn't good. Nothing about tonight was good. In fact, nothing about this week was good. Dinner with Joy in Manhattan had been troubling and he'd been on edge since, waiting for another call, wondering if he'd need to hop on a plane. "You haven't seen Alexandra, by chance?"

"Lost your girlfriend?" Benjamin asked, dunking a slice of California roll into soy sauce.

"Paige poured her cocktail all over Alexandra's dress."

"Paige?" Benjamin repeated, chewing the seaweed-wrapped roll.

"Your client Paige. The model."

"Ah, Paige." Benjamin smiled. "She's hot, isn't she?" Then he remembered himself and glanced around. "Where is Alexandra?"

Wolf nearly reached out to grab Benjamin by the throat. "That's what I'm asking you."

The lighting director from Wolf's last film joined them and reached for a piece of yellowfin sushi. "You're looking for your girl?" he said to Wolf.

Wolf nodded. "She'd gone to clean up her gown."

"I saw her," the lighting director said. "She's wearing an off-white gown, right?"

"Yes."

"She left," the lighting director said, reaching for another piece of sushi. "With Jason. I figured you two had a fight."

Wolf's features hardened. His dark eyes glittered. "There was no fight." He inhaled sharply as he saw red. "But there will be now."

And as Wolf headed to the front circular driveway, he prayed he'd find Alexandra at home. Alone. Because if Jason was there…

Wolf shook his head, not even wanting to finish the thought. Because he knew exactly what he'd do and it wouldn't be pretty.

Across town, Alexandra stood swaying in her living room, having finished changing into the little black cocktail dress she'd worn to Rye's birthday party at Spago. Jason had offered to make drinks for them while she changed, and she'd agreed.

He'd been so nice about driving her all the way to Culver City and patiently waiting while she rummaged through her closet trying to find something elegant to wear. But the cocktail was doing funny things to her, and she grabbed the living room wall for support.

"My head," she whispered, her body going cold all over and alarmingly tingly.

"Have a headache, doll?"

She didn't like his tone or the way he was looking at her. But Alexandra didn't close her eyes until the room started to spin. "What's going on?" she demanded huskily as soon as she could open her eyes again.

Jason was standing in front of her. "Hi, big eyes." He reached up, pushed a long lock of hair from Alex's eyes. "How are you feeling?"

"Dizzy."

"Are you? Maybe we need to get you to your bedroom so you can lie down."

"No." She put out a hand and immediately thought she'd fall. She needed Wolf here. She shouldn't have left Wolf. "Call…call…Wo-Wolf." She forced the words out, squinting her eyes to try to slow the spinning, but it didn't help. Nothing was working right. She wasn't working right.

"You don't need Wolf," Jason answered, taking her hand, fingers wrapping around hers. "I can help you. I'll get you into bed, don't worry."

"I need a doc-doctor. Call doctor."

"No, no, you'll be fine. I'll just take you to bed, darling."

"Call Wolf," she repeated, struggling to resist him as he dragged her toward the bedroom.

"You'll feel better in bed. Trust me."

She felt stiff, sick, puppetlike, her legs and arms disjointed. *"No."*

In her room, Jason closed her bedroom door and Alexandra's legs gave out. Jason pulled her up, pressed her against the wall. "One kiss, baby," he crooned.

It was then she realized how drunk he was—or drugged he was—because this wasn't the Jason she'd met at the studio office a month ago and this wasn't the Jason who offered to drive her home from the party.

But now this Jason was trying to kiss her, and the more she struggled to escape, the more excited he became.

"Stop it. Let me go," she choked out, turning her head away from his wet mouth.

"Why? You like me. I know you like me."

"No, I don't like you." Alexandra sucked in a breath, fighting to stop her head from spinning, fighting to regain strength in her limbs.

"Don't be that way," he answered, leaning against her, holding her immobile. "I want you. I'm crazy about you."

"Get off—"

But he'd cut her words off with another hard kiss that repulsed her so much her stomach turned inside out. He'd pinned her to the wall, his body leveraged against her, his knee slammed between her legs, his hands groping over her.

"Jason." She choked, violently twisting. *"Stop."*

But her struggles only enticed him, her shuddering body inflaming his. "Come on, Alex, kiss me," he whispered, grabbing at her face. "Kiss me properly. You know how."

But she wouldn't, she couldn't, just as she couldn't find the strength she needed to break away.

Wolf was nearing the front porch of Alex's small house when he heard the scream.

Alexandra.

Heart pumping, he took the three steps at one time. He was prepared to break the door down but was relieved to discover it'd been left unlocked. With a shove of his shoulder he had the door open.

In the bedroom, Alexandra screamed as Jason's hands slid across her.

"Come on, baby," Jason crooned, shifting his weight, and suddenly she felt his bare legs against her own as he battled to part her thighs.

He'd dropped his trousers.

She tried to scream again, but before she could make a sound, his head dipped and his mouth covered hers once more, smashing her nose, her mouth, cutting off air. Frantic, she bit savagely into Jason's lip, felt him stiffen even as she tasted a spurt of blood.

Stunned, Jason lifted his head and then his fist, and Alex squeezed her eyes shut, preparing to be hit, when suddenly Jason was off her, being hauled away by a massive, shadowed shape.

Even though the room was dark and spinning, even though she could barely see, much less stand, she knew it was Wolf.

Somehow she had known he would come.

"Alexandra." He ground out her name in the dark, and in his voice she heard fury that turned her blood cold.

An icy shiver raced up and down her spine. Wolf sounded angry enough to commit murder. "I'm okay," she choked out, pressing her black dress down, trying to cover the length of her bare legs. It was so odd, so strange. Her body could have been anybody's body. Her body didn't even seem to recognize her. She couldn't move from the wall, couldn't walk, couldn't function.

What in God's name was wrong with her?

And as she heard Wolf speak, his voice low and harsh, his accent stronger than she'd ever heard it, Alexandra fell back, hit the wall and slid all the way down, passing out before she touched the ground.

Alexandra was having a nightmare and she couldn't wake up. Someone, something, was hurting her, jabbing something down her throat, shoving something down into her middle. She tried to pull away but couldn't. Hands held her still. There was no relief.

And then she was gagging, vomiting, and she wasn't sure if it was real or a dream. The pain felt real enough, but nothing seemed clear, nothing made sense. But finally the gagging stopped and she was left alone and she slept.

While Alexandra slept, sedated, Wolf paced next to her bed. The doctor had said the drugs were finally out of her system thanks to gastric lavage with activated charcoal.

As Wolf paced, he watched her sleep but was far from calm. She hadn't liked having her stomach pumped, and when she woke, she'd be confused. She wouldn't remember much of last night.

Wolf clenched his teeth in mute outrage.

What was she thinking, going home with Jason?

His gut churned. Burned. His temper felt lethal.

He continued to pace, battling to contain his anger when all he wanted to do was find Jason and annihilate him. He could, too. He could make Jason suffer—and more.

Many successful screen and television actors were short, even slight, and they'd learned to use the camera close-up to their advantage, the zoom lens capturing carved jaws and handsome clefted chins.

But Wolf wasn't small or slight. He had the size and height of the professional boxer he'd once been. He'd made a name for himself in Ireland as the Dublin Devil—a furious, fire-fisted street fighter who leveled all his opponents within just one round. He hit that hard. His blows were that accurate.

And now he wanted to do what he did best—fight.

On the inside, he wasn't an actor, he was still an athlete, a boxer. Hollywood had never been in Wolf's sights. Being half Irish, he was as steeped in the great Irish literary tradition as the next snot-nosed kid, knew the Irish playwrights and poets and had seen his share of theater by the time he turned sixteen. But be in a play? Put on makeup, learn lines, be fitted by a costume designer? Never.

It wasn't until an independent film company from America came calling, looking to cast an Irish boxer in a small role in an even smaller film, that Wolf got noticed.

The casting director loved him, but the film couldn't find proper funding and never opened in theaters, going straight instead to America's booming cable business. But it turned out Wolf didn't need a box-office hit to turn his fifteen minutes of fame into a huge career.

Anyone who had seen the film had come away with two impressions—the script was a convoluted mess and the tall, dark, brooding boxer, Wolf Kerrick, was unforgettable.

A year and one finished major motion picture later, critics were falling over themselves, gushing praise.

Fast forward ten-plus years and he was even more of a Hollywood heavyweight than anyone imagined he'd ever be.

He'd certainly surpassed anything he'd ever dreamed he'd be. But then, he'd never dreamed. He'd wanted little. Preferred even less.

Growing up, his parents had fought bitterly, and their divorce when he was twelve had been something of a relief. At least the long, drawn out screaming matches had ended. There'd been no more broken dishes or doors. At first Wolf's dad had disappeared. But then, when Wolf's mom hadn't been able to take care of Wolf or even keep a job, his dad had abruptly returned and moved Wolf back to Ireland with him.

Wolf knew his dad wasn't a bad man, but his dad wasn't a talker, and the changes, coupled with silence, made a confused kid angry. But Wolf soon discovered he liked being angry. Anger gave him power, anger made him strong, anger gave him a reason to go to bed at night and then wake up the next morning.

Being angry had filled his days, fueled his runs, helped him train.

Being angry had allowed him to take hits and, even more importantly, dish it out. Angry, he could pound his opponents, mash them. Punish them.

Which is what he'd do to Jason as soon as he knew Alexandra would be fine.

Hours later, Alexandra slowly opened her eyes, stared up at the lavender-tinted ceiling above her. It was lavender, wasn't it? But why lavender?

She narrowed her eyes, trying to figure out where she was and why the ceiling would be this color. She didn't know anyplace with a ceiling like this or walls papered in soft swirlies of lavender, cream, gold and gray.

What ugly paper.

Looking the other way, she saw the table next to her bed with the plastic water pitcher and plastic cup and straw jostling for prominence among vases of flowers and sprays of white orchids.

Hospital.

She was in the hospital.

Alex tried to swallow but stopped when it hurt like hell.

Her throat was unbelievably sore and her stomach felt just as bad. There was an IV taped to the back of her left hand, and a black paper had been taped over the window in her door.

Why was she here? What was going on?

Alex stirred, turning onto her side to find the call button, but before she could push it the door to her room opened. Wolf entered, carrying a cup of coffee.

He looked at her, one eyebrow lifting ever so slightly. "You live."

"Barely," she croaked, watching him close the door and then approach her side.

He said nothing, and for a long moment neither did she, lying there against the stiff hospital pillow feeling fragile and strangely broken. She hurt, her insides hurt, and not knowing what had happened and not having anyone here but Wolf made her feel even more defenseless.

"Look at me. I don't know what happened," Alex whispered, vocal cords bruised. "Jason gave me a ride home to change so I could return to the party. While I was changing, he made us a drink and then—" She broke off, bit her cracked lower lip. "He…he…got weird."

"You were screaming when I arrived," Wolf finished roughly.

"I was scared." She closed her eyes, drew a deep breath. "Thank you for coming to look for me." Opening her eyes, she reached out, caught Wolf's pinkie finger between two of hers. "You saved me."

He said nothing, his head averted, his narrowed gaze fixed on the wall.

She tugged on his hand, trying to persuade him to look at her. "Thank you, Wolf."

Slowly his head turned and he gazed down at her, a deep furrow between his thick brows, his dark eyes more black than brown. "What if I hadn't come? What if I hadn't left the party when I did?"

She stared up into his eyes. The black depths burned. But it wasn't just anger blazing in his eyes. It was fear.

"But you did," she whispered.

"If I'd been five minutes later—"

"But you weren't." She squeezed his hand. "Please, let's forget about it."

Wolf abruptly pulled away. He walked from the bed, went to the window, where he looked out. "Forget?"

"Yes, forget. Move on. There's so much more that's important—"

"Not to me." He glanced at her over his shoulder. "God, you're so innocent! So naive. You were drugged. Attacked. You had an allergic reaction to the pharmaceutical cocktail he put in your drink. *Alexandra.*" His voice deepened, fell, vibrating with fury and outrage. "You could have *died* from the drugs alone."

Her heart thumped. She felt dizzy all over again. "I only had a drink with him, Wolf. I wouldn't take anything. I know it's dangerous."

"As we discovered."

"Please believe me."

He took a breath, his broad shoulders tensing, and then he exhaled in a slow, hard stream. "I believe you."

"You do?"

He nodded slowly, rubbed a hand over his eyes. "Jason likes to mix pills with his liquor—cocaine and temazepam are favorites of his." He fell silent a moment as he considered her. "Do you have family we should call? Someone I should contact?"

Her eyes widened. She shook her head. "There's no one," she whispered.

"You've no family?"

She stared up at him, terrified he'd discover the truth. No family? Alexandra had the most protective, overbearing family in the universe. "No."

"Do you want me to get you legal counsel then?"

"Legal counsel for what?"

"Because you'll want to press charges."

She was beginning to wish she hadn't woken up. This was too much, too overwhelming. "Do you want me to press charges?"

He exhaled in a harsh whoosh. "I don't know. I just want to beat the hell out of him. Want to make him—" He broke off, his beard-darkened jaw jutting tautly.

"Wolf, you could destroy him," breathed Alex. "And whatever he did, I don't want that."

He towered above her, his dark eyes frosted with ice, his features glacier-cold. "I would not be a man if I stood by and allowed him to go unpunished for hurting you."

"I won't let you! Someone has to think about your reputation. The press."

Wolf made a harsh sound in the back of his throat. "Press? You want to talk about press?" He laughed, but the sound was like fingernails down a chalkboard. "Alexandra, it's a little late to worry about bad press."

"What do you mean?"

"We're the topic of this morning's talk radio, and there was a blurb in the gossip section of the morning paper, too." He leaned over, kissed her forehead, his lips warm against the iciness of her skin. "And I can guarantee we'll be all over the news segments on the entertainment shows tonight," he murmured.

His words made her go numb all over. "What are they saying?"

"They're reporting that you were hospitalized for a drug overdose."

Her gaze lifted, found his. *"What?"*

"A photographer caught the ambulance wheeling you out of your house." He sighed. "The photo has me right there at your side."

"What is the paper saying?"

"You don't want to know."

She'd begun to tremble. "Tell me."

He hesitated so long she wasn't sure he would. And then he took her hand, lifted it to his mouth and kissed the backs of her fingers. "That you tried to kill yourself."

"Oh, my God."

His silence was deafening, and Alexandra closed her eyes, shrinking inwardly. All their joint efforts, everything they'd tried to do...gone.

Over.

"And this was in the paper?" she asked, imagining the reaction her family would have if they got word of this.

"Today's *Los Angeles Times.*"

She exhaled gradually, trying to calm herself. If it was just the *Los Angeles Times,* maybe none of her family would hear. None of her brothers lived in L.A. anymore.

"And *USA Today,*" Wolf added quietly.

Her stomach heaved. Her throat sealed closed. *USA Today* was a huge national paper. *"No."*

"No is right. Our publicity-stunt relationship has made headline news."

CHAPTER SEVEN

THEY KEPT ALEXANDRA for most of the day to give her suffi-
cient opportunity to rest and recover. They would have kept her
overnight again but Wolf feared that the media frenzy outside
would only grow if she wasn't discharged.

The hospital administration, as fed up with the paparazzi
as Wolf, allowed Alexandra to exit the hospital late that
evening from a side door into the waiting limousine,
avoiding the main entrance where photographers and reporters still lurked.

"You're not taking me home?" Alexandra said as the limousine left UCLA's medical center, traveled down Wilshire Boulevard to the 405 Freeway on-ramp.

"Not with those vultures watching your house."

"But I need clothes, pajamas, a toothbrush at least."

"You can manage one night without all that."

She pressed her lips together to hold back the protest. She
didn't have a leg to stand on anyway. She'd gotten them into
this mess, and Wolf, considering the circumstances, was
braving the spate of bad press very well.

Wolf's home in Malibu was tucked among other celebrity
homes, each hidden behind massive walls, shrubbery and gates.
It wasn't until the limo passed through the gates and around one
of the tall white stucco walls that the house, lit by a spotlight,
came into view.

The house, a sprawling modern cube with enormous

windows that faced the sea, was as serene as the beach and blue watery horizon beyond.

Wolf unlocked the front door and swung it open before stepping back to let her enter.

The surfaces were sleek, glass, chrome. The couches were low and white, oversize and covered in white chenille. The cocktail table and end tables were equally huge, low thick slabs of exotic wood hand carved and crafted. Even the walls— where there were walls—were plastered white, and the artwork was selective, modern oil paintings by some of the contemporary masters of the day. One painting, more violet than purple, hung above the smooth stucco fireplace. Another vast gray-and-pewter canvas hung on the opposite wall, above a Brazilian-wood console.

"Your room," he said, opening the door to a guest room down the hall from his. "And you can sleep in this," he added, tossing a large gray T-shirt in her direction.

"You've done this before," she answered, clumsily catching the T-shirt.

He acted as though he hadn't heard. "A new toothbrush is on the counter in your bath. Toothpaste is in the drawer. Fresh towels are on the towel rack."

Alexandra headed into the bathroom and, stripping off her clothes, took a long hot shower and worked at peeling off the adhesive strips from the IV that still remained on her arm.

Once finished, she dried off, tugged Wolf's T-shirt over her head and brushed her teeth.

When she left the bathroom, she saw that his bedroom door was now closed and she could hear him talking in a low voice on the phone. She overheard bits of the conversation, phrases like *Soon I'll be there* and *There'll be lots of time in Africa.*

Joy.

He was talking to Joy about shooting the movie in Africa because soon he'd be there. Another couple of weeks and he'd be on location.

With Joy.

Alexandra swallowed the stab of jealousy. Wolf had said

there'd been no affair, he'd said they were only friends, but somehow Joy and Wolf's relationship made her feel insecure. Like an outsider. Wolf and Joy were both actors and celebrated and beautiful, while she was…

Ordinary.

Sighing, Alexandra returned to her room, shut the door and climbed into the guest bed. It was a huge bed for a guest room and she felt very small in it.

The small feeling only grew worse as she struggled to relax. Sleep was a long time coming. She'd spent too much time in bed the past twenty-four hours as it was.

And as she lay there, thoughts churning, stomach in knots, she realized she wasn't just upset about Joy. She was also really upset with herself for thinking she could compete with Joy, live in Wolf's world without getting hurt.

Alexandra felt a bittersweet ache inside her chest, a tug on her heartstrings. Sometimes Wolf reminded her of the cowboy of her girlish dreams. He was every bit as big, and handsome and strong. Capable of looking out for her without smothering her. Sure enough to let her be without trying to change who she was or what she dreamed.

If only he were that hero…

If only those happy Hollywood endings really came true. But she knew better. Once you visited Los Angeles you realized that Hollywood wasn't a place but an intersection of streets. You realized that the golden sun in California postcards was rarely seen due to a disgusting layer of smog. *It's not that happy endings aren't possible in Hollywood,* Alexandra told herself, pulling her pillow close to her cheek, *it's just that they're highly unlikely.*

Alexandra thrashed in bed much of the night but woke up to the smell of freshly ground coffee and felt almost like a new woman.

Unable to face putting her party dress back on, Alexandra dragged her hands through her hair and headed to the kitchen in the gray T-shirt. Fortunately it was long on her, hitting her midthigh, and it covered her better than any silky baby-doll pajamas would.

It was Wolf in the kitchen making coffee, and when Alexandra appeared in the doorway he offered her a cup.

"Please," she answered, watching him take another big white glazed mug down from the glass-fronted cabinet.

He filled her cup, and she added a spoon of sugar before clasping the mug between both hands and taking a sip. It was strong and very good. "Thanks."

"My pleasure."

She took another sip and covertly watched him as he sliced several oranges and squeezed fresh juice into two tumblers. Once he finished with the juice he turned his attention to making toast.

"Butter, marmalade, strawberry jam?" he asked, rummaging through his huge stainless-steel refrigerator.

"Just butter," she answered, wondering exactly what his timeline was for getting her home. She'd missed work yesterday and now today was Saturday, and although she hadn't anything planned, she felt a need to establish some control again. Get back to her usual routine.

He grabbed the newspaper from the kitchen counter. "I always have my coffee outside on the deck. Care to join me?"

Her eyes narrowed a fraction. He was being polite. Too polite. Something was up. "Only if you'll share some of the newspaper," she answered, suddenly on guard.

His mouth curved. It wasn't a friendly smile. "Depends on the section."

She was beginning to think that she'd woken to a potentially explosive situation. "I like Arts & Leisure," she said.

"Yours." He held the glass door for her, and as Alexandra stepped outside she blinked at the bright morning sunshine. Here in Malibu the sky was blue and the sun was shining and long, smooth bottle-green waves crashed on the white beach.

She took the seat he offered and he divided the newspaper, but unlike Wolf, she didn't start reading. She watched him for several minutes, curious that he could be so absorbed in the paper when life seemed so confusing. "Wolf."

"Hmm?"

"Are we going to talk about what happened?"

"No," he answered without looking up.

Seagulls swooped low overhead and her stomach thumped with nerves. "Why not?"

"Because there's nothing to discuss."

She pulled her section of the paper closer to her but still couldn't read. Sitting outside on the deck, drinking coffee, sharing the paper, watching the seagulls and listening to the waves break, they looked like a typical Malibu couple, and theirs was such a normal domestic scene, that Alexandra found herself hoping that maybe, just maybe, yesterday's headlines had already been forgotten.

That no one remembered her suicide attempt from a drug overdose.

She exhaled, the stream of air blowing a wisp of hair up and out of her eyes.

She hoped…until she glanced up from the paper and spotted a photographer on the beach with a camera focused in their direction. Her heart fell with a sickening thud. "There's a photographer on the beach."

"Really?" Wolf asked, turning the page in the paper. He didn't sound surprised or worried.

"You knew?" she demanded.

He folded the paper in half, glanced up at her, his expression shuttered. "There is always someone somewhere, lurking with a camera. You learn to get used to it, ignore the cameras as best as you can and get on with life."

She stared at him suspiciously. "You're sure we're not here for a photo op? A get-well shot for the paparazzi?"

He smiled grimly. "It's a nice idea. I wish I'd thought of it." He folded the paper yet again so it was a quarter of its original size. "As it happens, this is my house and this is the deck where I have breakfast every morning. And you, Alexandra, just happen to be here." He returned to his paper and resumed reading, but Alex couldn't read—or focus.

"They think I was distraught over Joy, don't they?" she whispered, holding her large ceramic mug between both hands.

"Mmm."

"But you weren't even with Joy at the party," Alexandra continued faintly, staring at the top of his head because that's all he'd give her.

"No," he answered, face still buried in the *Times*. "But getting the facts right isn't a priority for the tabloids. They're concerned with selling newspapers, not the truth—" He broke off as the phone began to ring in the house. "Let me grab that. It could be the studio. The producers are holding an emergency meeting this morning. They're discussing recasting the lead roles for the film. Sometime in the next hour we'll find out if it's me or Joy that's being replaced."

Alexandra's eyes widened with alarm. "Oh, Wolf—"

"Please don't." He paused in the doorway as the phone continued to ring. "It's too late for that, Alexandra. Let's just enjoy what's left of the morning, shall we?"

Alexandra watched Wolf hang up the phone and open the door and walk toward her where she still sat outside. "Bad news?" she asked quietly.

He didn't answer. He just stared down at her. "You're always so curious, so full of questions," he said thoughtfully. "Maybe it's time I got to know you better."

His expression filled her with unease. "What do you want to know?" she asked, trying to find a smile. He was acting strangely, had been acting strangely all morning, but the phone call had only heightened the tension another notch.

"Who you really are."

Her mouth opened to protest and then she snapped it closed. She owed him no explanations. They might have a contract, but it was going to end soon. Wolf would be leaving in two weeks for Africa, and once he was gone he'd be out of her life for good.

"Do I get to go home soon?" she asked, standing, wanting to put herself on more equal footing.

"Mmm...no."

"Why not?" she asked, trying to keep her tone reasonable. Maybe if she humored him, he'd finally send her back to her house.

"I've a lunch date and I'd very much like your company."

She glanced down at his gray T-shirt she was still wearing and then at her bare feet. "I have to go home to change. I've nothing here to wear."

"Benjamin is sending the stylist."

Alexandra stilled. "That was Benjamin on the phone?"

"Mmm."

Wolf's ambiguous answers were beginning to trouble her. "What's going on, Wolf?"

"Lunch."

"Why lunch?" she persisted, arms folding across her chest, pulling the T-shirt taut across her breasts.

His gaze dropped, sweeping slowly across the outline of her breasts and the pebbled nipples. He smiled, his cool, fierce, predatory smile. "I'm hungry," he answered. "And we need to do some damage control."

An hour and ten minutes later they were in Wolf's navy Lamborghini, a classic V12 sports car from the late '60s. It was the same car Wolf had originally picked her up in for their first official date as a couple at Casa Del Mar's Veranda lounge.

Alexandra had fun that night but somehow she didn't think she'd be having fun today.

As Wolf drove down Highway 1 south toward Los Angeles, Alexandra smoothed the snug skirt on her gray Michael Kors dress the stylist had brought her. The dress was fitted with thin spaghetti straps, a plunging sweetheart neckline and a beautiful black lace-and-satin-ribbon belt at the waist. Her heels were black, her clutch was black and her thick hair had been curled and left loose.

She looked great. Sexy. Polished. She should have been confident.

She wasn't.

"Where are we going to lunch?" she asked, fixing one of the delicate gold hoops at her ears. It'd twisted and caught in her hair.

"Asia de Cuba," he answered, briefly taking his eyes off the road.

Asia de Cuba, she silently repeated, crossing her legs and noting that her French pedicure could use a touch-up. "I don't know that place."

"It's a nice restaurant."

"Where is it?"

Wolf shot her a sideways glance. "My, you're curious today."

Alex shifted uncomfortably in the Lamborghini's low white leather seat and recrossed her legs the other way. "You're acting strange."

"Am I?"

Her jaw flexed as her gaze rested on him. Something was definitely up. "Secretive," she added.

"Really?"

She let the subject go for now. He obviously wasn't in a talkative mood and she didn't feel like playing games. Her lashes dropped, concealing her anxiety as the miles sped past. They were on the Santa Monica Freeway now, heading toward Hollywood.

"What are you not telling me?" she asked tersely. She didn't like Wolf like this, didn't like it when he played the famous actor card and made her feel like a walk-on part in his Broadway play. "You're acting as if you know something that I don't. Something that maybe I should."

"Indeed." Wolf shifted, accelerated, taking the steep curve of Sunset Boulevard fast. "And I've thought about telling you, but maybe I should just let you enjoy the surprise."

Surprise. So there was something about to happen. She exhaled, her nerves so on edge that she didn't think she'd be able to sit still another moment longer. "Why do I get the feeling this isn't going to be a good surprise?"

Wolf shrugged, glanced up into his rearview mirror to check the traffic behind him, including the police car that had settled behind them in their lane. "I suppose it all depends on how you feel about family get-togethers."

"Families are fine." Alexandra's stomach was back in free-fall form. "I didn't realize you had family in town."

"I don't."

She knew then, but she didn't want to know, didn't want to have her worst fears confirmed. "Then who?"

He pulled into the hotel drive which fronted the famous Sunset Strip. The Mondrian Hotel was within steps of some of the best restaurants, clubs and nightlife Los Angeles offered. He glanced at her as they approached the hotel, the Mondrian's entrance marked by a pair of massive decorative mahogany doors that soared thirty feet into the air. "Two men by the names of Troy and Trey."

Alexandra felt a shot of icy adrenaline shoot through her, pumping her veins full of cold silver liquid fear. Wolf couldn't have just said what he said. He couldn't know their names. There was no way...

Wolf heard her faint choking sound and gave her an appraising look. "Those names ring a bell, love?"

The hotel loomed closer; elegant, white and spare, it was said to be designed to remind guests of the famous Los Angeles fog that covered the city when the weather grew warm.

"Troy and Trey are my brothers," she said unsteadily. Her hands twisted in her lap even as she caught the lift of Wolf's eyebrow.

"The twins," she amended huskily.

"And just how many brothers do you have?"

"Five."

"Five," he echoed softly. "Out of how many kids?"

"Six."

"You're the only girl."

She nodded.

"And the youngest," he concluded.

She nodded again.

"So what was this about not having any family, Alexandra?" He'd pulled over to the hotel curb and shifted into park, but the engine still ran and he ignored the cream-suited valet attendant hovering outside.

She would have slunk down lower in her seat if she could. "You're an only child," she said hoarsely. "You wouldn't understand."

"Try me."

"There's five of them." She swallowed, pressed her hand over her stomach, feeling the nervous nausea start up again. She'd always had a weak stomach, everything used to make her queasy. She'd thought she'd beaten the childish impulse, but since meeting Wolf the feeling seemed to be back all the time. "And I don't know if you've met the twins yet, but they're all like that. Big, tough, no-nonsense, just like my dad and granddad."

"I haven't met the twins," Wolf answered, finally turning the key in the ignition. "But they're determined to see you. And me." He paused, considered her. "Apparently they're quite worried about you."

She tipped her head back against the buttery-soft leather seat and closed her eyes even as she gripped the door handle so tightly she felt as though the bones in her hand would break. "Don't make me go in there. Don't make me see them."

"They love you."

Alexandra heard Wolf open his door and she leaned forward, caught at his hand. "They love me too much," she said, holding tightly to his wrist. "And after Mom died it only got worse."

The valet attendant had opened her door and was standing beside her, waiting for her to step out, but neither she nor Wolf paid him any attention.

"They can't be bad brothers if they've flown here looking for you."

"Yes, they've rushed here." Her hand wrapped tighter around his wrist. "To bring me home."

"You don't know that."

"But I do," she insisted. Ever since she was little her brothers had been so protective that it'd suffocated her. They wouldn't let her do anything on her own. They hadn't wanted her to go away to college either. "I'm not going back." She lifted her head, met Wolf's dark gaze. "They can say what they want, do what they want. But I'm not going home. I'm staying here with you."

Wolf had heard a lot of ludicrous things in his life, touching things, too. At thirty-five, he thought he'd pretty much heard everything. But in all these years he'd never met anyone quite like Alexandra.

She was unique. An original.

"Why would you want to stay with me?" he teased. "You don't even like me."

Two pink spots burned high in her cheeks. "Maybe. But you're the only one I know who can stand up to them."

Wolf slipped out from her grasp and walked around to the passenger side, where he extended his hand to Alexandra. "A loving family like that only wants the best for you."

"Sure. I could go back to Montana and the Lazy L ranch and get married and have babies and wouldn't that be an exciting life?"

Wolf had to check his smile as he drew an extremely unwilling Alexandra to her feet. "Life on a ranch has to be a lot more interesting than that."

"Oh, yeah. Horses. Cows. It's just great."

"Benjamin said your brothers are big. Is that how they got their size? Chasing horses and cows around?"

It was her turn for the corners of her lips to curve. "All Shanahans are big."

Wolf took the car's claim check from the valet attendant before putting his arm around Alexandra to steer her through the huge mahogany doors and into the hotel's vast glossy white lobby. "So what happened to you?"

Her soft, husky laugh suddenly died as two enormous men stepped from the cool white sheer curtains floating everywhere.

Alexandra stiffened and froze. "Trey," she breathed unsteadily. "Troy."

CHAPTER EIGHT

THE BROTHERS SHANAHAN wasted no time getting to the point.

"We'd like a word alone with our sister," Trey said, and while his voice was quiet, his tone brooked no argument.

"I want Wolf to stay," Alexandra replied, reaching in panic for Wolf's hand.

"Alexandra, this is a matter for family," Troy said, shooting Wolf a far from friendly look.

"Yes, but Wolf is like family," she answered, holding his hand even tighter. She knew her brothers, knew they weren't the sort to mince words, and they weren't mincing any now.

Troy's expression became ever more suspicious as he stared Wolf down. "Then he should be protecting you, not hurting you," he said. "Because we don't like hearing you've been hospitalized any better than Dad or the others do."

Alexandra's hand was damp and it felt sticky clenching Wolf's hand, but she couldn't let go. "It's not what you think."

"No? Then explain it," Trey demanded.

She caught how Wolf's dark eyes flashed and his jaw clenched. He didn't like Trey's tone and he was fighting to control his temper.

Hotel guests glanced at them curiously as they crossed through the lobby, with its flutter of white curtains and the floating wall of elevators. The lobby, with its all-white surfaces, had a surreal beauty, reminding Alexandra more of an art gallery.

The slick and smooth white finishes and furnishings were designed to instill calm, but it wasn't working on anyone in their little group.

"Alexandra, we're worried about you," Troy said bluntly. "We've talked to Dad and we're here to take you home."

She wasn't surprised. This was how Shanahans handled things. They came, they conquered, they went.

"I'm not going home," she answered quietly, standing as tall she could manage considering that, as more than one person had said to her when she was growing up, the twins could pass for mountains.

"Well, I'm not leaving you here," Trey growled, his square jaw growing thicker by the second.

She gazed up at him and then at Troy, torn between admiration and exasperation. Her brothers were good-looking, damn good-looking, without an ounce of fat on them. They were made of hard, honed muscle that wrapped their arms and legs like steel and they were every bit as rigid.

Her smile was bittersweet. "Trey, you don't have a choice." She'd once enjoyed fighting with them, stirring her brothers up, trying to get a rise from them, but things were different now. The stakes were far higher. "This is my home—"

"That's absurd," Troy interrupted roughly. "Home is the Lazy L ranch, home is Dad, Brock, the kids."

She shook her head, aware of Wolf standing there, just behind her shoulder. She was grateful to have him with her and even more grateful he was letting her handle this her way. "Not anymore."

Trey cleared his throat, making a rough sound of disgust. "You're telling me the ranch isn't home?"

She looked from Trey to Troy and back. The twins had the same jaw, the same high cheekbones, the same blue eyes as clear as the Montana sky. "I'm sorry you've had a wasted trip. But tell Dad I'm fine. Tell him I'll try to come home for Christmas—"

"You'll come to Montana and tell him yourself," Troy interrupted brusquely, folding his arms, pulling the fabric of his white dress shirt even tauter. The snug fabric shaped the width of his chest and the thick biceps and triceps in his arms. "And while you're there, be sure to explain just how it was that you nearly died, because we know all about it. We know you were rushed to the hospital, had your stomach pumped and kept for a day under observation."

Alexandra felt Wolf's warmth and presence. She wasn't sure if he'd taken a step toward her or she'd taken a step back, but she could feel him there—his size, his strength, his fierce personality—and again it reassured her. All her life her brothers had trampled over her wishes, but this time having Wolf in her corner settled her. Gave her confidence. "What you heard, what you read in the paper was a mistake," she said carefully. "It's not what really happened."

"So you didn't try to kill yourself?" Troy demanded, voice dropping to a husky growl. "Because that nearly broke Dad's heart. He loves you more than the five of us boys put together."

Troy might as well have stabbed her with an ice pick, she thought, lips parting in silent protest as tears filled her eyes. The idea of her dad worrying about her, suffering because of her, was more than she could bear. "I'll call him," she said softly, her voice breaking. "I'll call him tonight."

Trey loomed over her. "You'll go home tonight and you'll talk to him in person. Properly. The way you should."

She felt rather than saw Trey's finger jabbing at her, emphasizing his disgust. She swiped away a tear, livid with him, both of them, realizing all over again why she'd left home. She loved her brothers and hated her brothers and couldn't understand how any relationship could be so complicated. They protected her and disciplined her and talked at her until she felt absolutely trapped.

She angrily wiped away another tear. "I never tried to kill myself. The media got it wrong. Somebody was being funny and put something in my drink."

Troy and Trey exchanged thunderous glances. "What kind of lifestyle is this?" Trey snapped. "You're too thin, too tan, too made-up. You're not Alex at all."

"I am," she protested.

"You're not," Troy said more gently. "You're some Hollywood paper doll. But that's not who Dad raised you to be, and Mom wouldn't be proud either."

Every word her brothers said hurt, but this last, this condemnation that her mother wouldn't have approved, cut her to the quick. She looked away, eyes closing, stunned by the depth of her pain.

She couldn't do this anymore, couldn't take this anymore. She turned to Wolf, put her hand on his forearm. "I want to go," she whispered. "Can we please just go?"

His narrowed gaze swept her tear-streaked face. "Of course. Whatever you want."

But before they could take two steps, Trey reached out, grabbed Alexandra's arm. "And what will I tell Dad?"

Wolf swiftly knocked Trey's hand from Alexandra's arm. His features contorted. "Don't touch her like that again. She's a woman, not one of your cows."

Trey's expression darkened. "She's my sister, and I love her and I want what's best for her."

"If you want what's best," Wolf answered evenly, "then tell your father she's happy and doing well in Los Angeles with me."

"With you," Troy repeated icily.

"And just who the hell are you to make decisions for Alexandra?" Trey asked, hands knuckling to fists.

Alexandra knew the twins were formidable opponents. Just like armored tanks, they rolled right over their opposition, and she sensed they were going to roll right now.

"Your sister's fiancé," Wolf answered quietly. "We're engaged to be married." He looked from one to the other. "Didn't you know?"

"Engaged?" Trey could barely get the word out, and Alexandra couldn't meet his eye, too shocked to think of a single thing to say.

Wolf, her fiancé? Engagement? Oh, how quickly this had escalated.

Troy pointed to her bare left hand. "There's no ring."

"It's still secret," Wolf said, smiling faintly. He seemed to have no problem with the story and looked downright amused by her brothers' sudden tailspin.

Alexandra struggled to think of something to say, but her mind was strangely blank. Everything had been fine until Paige spilled the drink on her gown, but that one spilled drink had consequences she couldn't have dreamed of.

Ruined dress. Lethal cocktail. Headline news. Now an engagement to Wolf. Amazing how fast one problem had snowballed into this!

"Secret," Troy was repeating, lower lip curling. He might have moved from Montana to Seattle and exchanged horses for fast cars, but he was still a very tough cowboy underneath. "What kind of bullshit is this about a secret engagement?" he demanded, rocking back on his heels. "Why keep it quiet? Are you ashamed of her?

"Where we come from, Shanahans are respected, and so Alexandra has always been respected," he continued. "Maybe this is Hollywood. Maybe you think you're so special you can treat Alexandra any way you want, but you've got another think coming. Alexandra's a good girl, the sweetest girl you'll ever meet, and she deserves to be treated right."

The entire time Troy was talking, Wolf was looking at Alexandra, one black eyebrow half cocked. She struggled to maintain a pinched, if not terrified, smile.

As Troy fell silent, the corner of Wolf's mouth tilted in a dry smile. "The only reason it's secret is that I haven't had a chance to ask your father for Alexandra's hand yet."

"You're going to ask him?" Troy asked bluntly.

"Yes," Wolf answered.

"When?"

Wolf's brows drew together. "That's really none of your business, is it?"

"I hope you're serious," Trey growled, "because Alexandra doesn't deserve to have her heart stepped on."

Alexandra would have laughed if the situation weren't so serious. It'd been four years since she left home, but Trey and Troy were still the same. They used to threaten the local guys if they came near her. Little Alexandra was too good to be touched. Little Alexandra was a nice girl, a sweet girl, a virgin. She shuddered inwardly, remembering.

If she didn't have any experience when she came to Los Angeles it was because her brothers had made sure that no man came near her. Apparently Dillon had put a bounty on the head of anybody who tried to get too friendly with his baby sister. And in her brother Dillon's mind, anything past first base was too friendly.

Trey reached into his pocket, drew out his wallet. "How much would it take to get rid of you? Five million? Ten? What do you want?"

Alexandra blanched, the blood draining from her face. *"Trey."*

"Name your price," Troy echoed.

"My price?" Wolf's hard, cynical expression bordered on incredulous. "You think I can be bought?"

"We're willing to try." Troy wasn't the least bit apologetic. "We want you gone."

"That's pretty obvious. But my relationship with Alexandra has nothing to do with you, and the only one who has a say in how we proceed with our engagement—" Wolf paused, looked pointedly at Alexandra "—is your sister."

They were all looking at her now, waiting for her to respond. Her mouth dried and she licked her lips, trying to find her voice. Maybe it didn't matter that she couldn't find her voice, because she didn't have the foggiest idea of what to say.

"Is it true?" Trey asked roughly. "Is this your dream man? This is who you want to marry?"

Alexandra's gaze clung to Wolf's. They'd find a way out of this one later—they'd have to—but for now she'd do anything to keep her brothers from dragging her back to Montana. Montana wasn't home anymore, hadn't been home for years. "Yes."

"So when's the wedding?" Troy persisted.

"Soon," Wolf replied, taking Alexandra's hand in his and kissing the back of her fingers. "We'd planned to elope, marry on location in Zambia."

"Zambia?" Troy spluttered.

"Marry Alexandra in Africa?" Trey thundered. "That's not going to happen. No way. Not a snowball's chance in hell."

Troy's square jaw hardened, his blue eyes splintering with cool shards of light. "If you're going to marry her, you marry her here, where her family can attend. Do you understand?"

Wolf's own jaw firmed, but wry amusement touched his eyes. "Hard not to. You have such a way with words."

Glancing down into Alexandra's pale face, he smiled a small, mocking smile. "It's a California wedding."

They never did have lunch, and Alexandra found the long drive back to Wolf's house nothing short of agonizing. Wolf was beyond quiet. He looked like the Grim Reaper at the wheel. She did her best to avoid looking at him, but even with the sun shining and the temperature outside in the seventies, Alexandra couldn't stop shivering.

Wolf had promised her brothers a California wedding.

In less than two weeks.

A wedding in less than two weeks. That was laughable. Hilarious. So why wasn't she laughing?

Why did she want to cry?

Alexandra squeezed her eyes shut as her teeth began to chatter. It was just the shock, she told herself. As soon as she and Wolf figured a way out of this mess, she'd be fine. They just needed to put their heads together and come up with a plan.

Fast.

"Take a hot bath when we get home," Wolf said, merging into traffic on Highway 1. They were probably just ten or fifteen minutes from his house now. "Or better yet, I can turn on the hot tub for you. It's just off the deck in the garden. Has a great view of the water. That might help your chill."

She bundled her arms across her chest. "We've got to think of a way out of this, something plausible, something that will keep my family out of Los Angeles and away from me."

Wolf gave her a peculiar look. "Were you not at the Mondrian with me? Did you not hear what I heard? Those brothers aren't going away until you're married. They're taking hotel rooms in town and camping out until the dirty deed is done."

And that just might be why she was violently shivering. She was doomed. Wolf, too.

"I'm sorry," she whispered. "I'm really sorry about all of this. If I'd just stayed at the party, none of this would have happened."

"Celebrity is a messy business."

Alex grimaced. Talk about cold comfort. "So what do we do now?"

"We get married."

"You mean *pretend* to get married."

Wolf shot her a darkly amused glance. "Your brothers don't strike me as the pretend type, and frankly pretending has gotten us into this mess. I think it's time we sorted things out properly. A real wedding with a real priest, real guests and real champagne."

Which meant real publicity, too, she thought, stifling a groan.

The PR game had completely taken over her life, and she didn't like it. She'd didn't even know who she was anymore, what with the stylists and designers and makeup artists constantly fixing her up, making her presentable. She was ready for the old Alexandra to return. The one that went to work every day on time, slept seven and a half hours every night and wore black, navy and gray because that way people might take her seriously.

Lately she'd actually begun to miss just being ordinary.

"I think this has gone far enough, Wolf, don't you?" she asked quietly.

"If I did, I wouldn't have just proposed."

She ground her teeth in mute irritation. "It wasn't much of a proposal."

"Apparently I am your dream man."

She could have screamed with vexation. "That was a mistake."

"One your brothers latched onto." He signaled a lane change as they neared the house. "I imagine they've already been in contact with your dad by now."

Alexandra pressed her fists against her eyes. She didn't want to hear any more, didn't want to picture her brothers on the phone with her dad. Because Wolf was right. That's exactly what Troy and Trey would have done. Called Dad. Then called Brock, Dillon and Cormac. They'd all be jumping on airplanes soon.

"If I got down on one knee, would you feel any better?" Wolf asked without the least bit of sympathy for her plight.

She lifted her head, glared at him. *"No."*

He shrugged and turned down the small green-hedge-lined lane leading to his beach house. "Exactly. So why bother with the theatrics?"

No two weeks had ever passed faster, and no elaborate, star-studded wedding had ever been planned so quickly. Wolf made a few calls to industry insiders, and within a day the wedding ceremony was set, the reception site booked. Within three days the myriad details—including guest list, bridal gown, colors, flowers, dinner menu and entertainment—had been addressed. And by the fourth day the hand-embossed wedding invitations were sent.

Alexandra laughed until she cried when she received an invitation to her own wedding.

It was all so horrible it was funny.

She, Alexandra Shanahan, who'd lost a lot of sleep at fifteen fantasizing about Wolf Kerrick, was now marrying him in Santa Barbara in little over a week.

Santa Barbara, a ninety-minute drive north of Los Angeles on Highway 1, perches snugly between the Santa Ynez Mountains and the gorgeous Pacific Ocean. The town, a mixture of red-tiled adobe homes, huge estates and historic landmarks, also has some of the best surfing in California. Little wonder that everyone from John Travolta to Oprah Winfrey has a second home there.

And now Alexandra was about to be married there.

Pacing her small dressing room at the Denzinger estate, she kept glancing at the little clock on her dressing room table. Just a half hour now until the ceremony began.

She trembled in her white satin beaded shoes.

She couldn't believe Wolf was insisting they go through with the wedding. There was no reason to get married. Wolf could just head to Africa and she could make excuses, claim cold feet, lack of compatibility. Anything but marriage!

Alexandra marched back across the carpet and stole yet another look at the clock. Twenty-five minutes.

Twenty-five minutes until she became his wife.

And Alexandra, who hated to cry, knew she was about to cry now. Not delicate tears but huge, depressed sobs.

Until now she had always thought of herself as the ultimate cynic, a bona fide nonromantic. She didn't believe in falling in love, had never felt an urge to marry or to be a mother for some guy's children. But now, confronted by a very public wedding to a man she still barely knew, Alexandra was aghast.

She couldn't believe she was marrying to seal a business deal, to propel herself higher up the ladder of success. Even for a cynic, this was a really big deal.

Even for a cynic, this was wrong.

She couldn't do this. Not for Wolf, not for her family, not for anyone. She needed to get out of here, escape before she made a fool of herself in front of every guest and every camera.

Alex stopped pacing, turned, pressed a knuckled fist to her mouth, forgetting her carefully applied lipstick.

She didn't like running away, but she didn't know how else to get out of this. Her family certainly wasn't going to listen. And Wolf…well, he was heading to Zambia day after tomorrow. He'd be fine.

Glancing down, she took in her full white gown, a fairy-tale dress for a fairy-tale wedding that she refused to let happen.

She reached for the back of her gown, tried to tug the hooks open, but there were too many—absolutely dozens—hidden in a satin-lined seam in her dress. She couldn't undress without assistance, and there was no one she could ask to help.

If she wanted to go, she'd have to leave like this.

Alexandra crossed to her travel tote bag tucked between the vanity and the corner of the room. She checked inside for her wallet. With a sigh of relief she saw it was there. Good. For a moment she'd feared all her cash and credit cards would be, with her luggage, already at the hotel.

Alex grabbed her wallet and left the rest.

She'd just buy what she needed whenever she got wherever she was going, because she certainly couldn't go back to her house in Culver City. She wasn't even sure she'd have a job waiting for her after she stood Wolf up at the altar. But those were problems she'd worry about later.

Alexandra left the changing room, slipping quietly down the mansion's long sunlit corridor, away from the spacious public rooms to the working quarters of kitchen, laundry and garage.

She passed several uniformed housemaids but didn't make eye contact, too intent on getting away before someone checked on her in the bridal dressing room and discovered her gone.

She turned one corner and then another, then spotted a severe-looking door at the end of this last hallway. With a push she was through the door, out, free.

The sky above was still bright blue with warm fingers of sunlight despite the late afternoon hour. In another hour the sun would be slipping toward the ocean, but for now everything was clear and warm and sunny, a picture-perfect California day.

Alex's fingers squeezed the wallet as her white satin heels crunched the pea gravel. An antique Rolls Royce waited, decorated with a lavish amount of white ribbon and a white floral display. The getaway car, she thought with a shudder, passing it so quickly her full starched skirts pressed against one shiny hub.

"Can I help you find something?" a dark, laconic voice drawled from behind her, and Alex stiffened, disbelief sweeping through her, turning her blood to ice.

Slowly, painfully she turned and faced Wolf where he leaned against the side of the brick building. Her throat worked. No words would come out. He was the last person she'd expected to see out here.

"Looking for a pay phone?" he asked, indicating her wallet.

She shook her head, the lace veil creeping forward to caress her cheek.

"Missing family? Your stylist? Makeup artist?" One black eyebrow arched as he supplied excuse after excuse.

She tensed, her insides already a fury of knots and misery. "I was looking for a cab."

He said nothing for a moment, intently studying her frozen expression. "Running away, are you?"

"I never *agreed* to marry you. I never—"

"You didn't deny it when I told your brothers we were engaged, that we were getting married. You told them—"

"I was scared!"

"As you should have been. In fact, you should have been scared weeks before when you agreed to sign a contract to play my lover. If you're such a nice, inexperienced girl, what in God's name are you doing with me?"

Her eyes grew rounder. She swallowed convulsively. Her hair, curled in long spirals, danced across her back.

He was bearing down on her, huge, powerful in the jet-black tuxedo with the starched white shirt and white tie. "But when your family arrives like some vengeful Celtic warlord, I am not going to forget my responsibility to you. I am not going to walk away from you."

He stood tall over her, so tall she had to tip her head back to see his dark, angry eyes. "And you, Alexandra, are not going to walk away from me."

CHAPTER NINE

THE RECEPTION, LIKE the wedding, was a blur of lavender and rose and gold, of helicopters droning overhead and the sea crashing on rocks below. The wind kept catching at Alexandra's veil, blowing it up and down.

Now that the ceremony was over, she was glad she hadn't been able to hear the minister. It helped lessen the impact of his words, helped her focus instead on the future, the far distant future when she'd be someone—not because she'd married someone powerful, influential, but because she herself was powerful. Influential.

The guests kept flocking to meet her during the dinner reception. Being Wolf Kerrick's new blushing bride suddenly catapulted her to a position of importance. Whereas at Spago and the Silverman birthday party she'd been no one worth noting, now everyone wanted to greet her, and she air-kissed celebs, hugged actresses she'd never met and took dozens of smiling photographs with the industry's top execs.

It's a shame she hadn't won everyone over on her own merit, but at least the crowd's warmth and enthusiasm reassured the Shanahan men that their only girl had done okay for herself.

In fact, by the time Alexandra danced with her father, the men in her family had become Wolf Kerrick's newest, biggest fans.

Something Alexandra found painful as well as annoying.

The reception, like the ceremony, was held in the Denzinger garden, and the colors of the wedding were the same colors of the blue horizon, where the setting sun painted the ocean shades of lavender, rose and gold. A perfect Hollywood set for a perfect Hollywood film. But this was real.

The reception swept past her in a kaleidoscope of toasts and kisses, hugs and best wishes. There was dinner and then that nerve-racking first dance, the cake and the tossing of the garter. All the traditional things one did at an American wedding.

Wolf was now drawing her back onto the dance floor. He'd just been in conversation with her father—again.

"You and Dad seem to have found a lot in common," she said through gritted teeth as Wolf spun her around the floor in a grand Strauss waltz.

"He's fascinating," Wolf said.

"Maybe you're just trying to make points."

"Maybe," he agreed, twirling her around. "And you should smile, because he's watching right now and he really wants his little girl to be happy."

Alexandra stepped intentionally on his toe. "Oops!"

His hand settled lower on her back. "I didn't realize my love was quite so clumsy."

She offered him another dazzling but vacant smile. "I guess you don't really know me either."

The orchestra was playing with great gusto as they only had one more number before they ended their set, giving way to the R & B band.

"You understand this is for the cameras only, right?" Alexandra made sure everyone could see her teeth in her wide smile. "I'm playing a part, a role, and getting paid for it. Don't think for a moment that I'm actually attracted to you."

His smile revealed amusement. "But you are."

"No."

"You were."

"No."

"Love, I'm an actor, not stupid."

Alexandra tried to hold herself apart and aloof from him, but the strength in his grip made it increasingly difficult.

"We've met before," he added, spinning her around the floor, thoroughly enjoying the waltz. "Remember?"

She stared at his chin, afraid to look higher.

"It was about four years ago," he continued. "We met at the Beverly Hills Hotel in the Polo Lounge. You were with friends and—"

"I don't remember," she interrupted tersely, glancing wildly up, meeting his mocking dark gaze before glancing even more swiftly away.

"We passed each other in the hallway. I was just coming from the men's room and you were on your way to the ladies' room—"

"I don't remember," she interrupted breathlessly.

His lips curved ever so slightly. "We left the hotel together."

"No—"

"Went to the Ivy for dinner."

Her body felt cold all over and she'd stopped protesting now.

"After dinner we parked high up in the Hollywood Hills with a view of the entire valley."

Alexandra stared. He'd known. He'd known who she was all along. He'd known this entire time.

His dark gaze found hers, held. "How could you think I wouldn't remember you?"

Wordlessly she searched his face, trying to understand what he'd been thinking. "But I was heavier by nearly twenty pounds."

"I don't remember that."

Again she searched his eyes. "What do you remember?"

"Your sweetness, your intelligence, your humor—" he broke off, assessed the impact his words were having on her "—and your incredible inexperience."

When she couldn't manage to even squeak a protest, he dropped his head, kissed the curve of her ear and whispered, "A girl who didn't even know how to unzip a man's pants, give a hand job or perform oral sex. Now that's a girl to take home to meet Mom."

Alexandra shoved hard on his chest, abruptly ending the waltz. "You *remember*."

Grooves bracketed his firm lips. His lips curved, but it wasn't a tender smile. He reached for her, pulling her back into his arms and dipping his head. He kissed below her ear, in the small, delicate hollow where a pulse beat wildly, erratically. "Of course I remember."

His voice dropped even lower, so husky, so sensual it hummed all the way through her. "You couldn't possibly think that I'd marry just any woman. Could you, Alexandra?"

It was well after midnight before they were finally able to break away from the reception, which had turned into the party of the year. The wedding planners had arranged surprise appearances by several of the guests who happened to be top *Billboard* recording artists performing their hit songs, and everyone was dancing, including Alexandra, who suddenly felt as if she were the most popular girl in America.

But by the time she climbed into the waiting Rolls Royce, her satin beaded shoes had blistered nearly every toe on her feet and rubbed her heels raw. She'd tried taking her shoes off, but her full wedding gown was too long and she'd ended up tripping so many times she'd inadvertently pulled the bustled raw silk train down.

There was no traffic at such a late hour, and the drive from the Denzinger estate to the historic Four Seasons Biltmore, the premier hotel in Santa Barbara nestled in the exclusive Montecito enclave, was short. So short that Alexandra didn't even have a chance to get her head around the fact that tonight she and Wolf were sharing a room.

Despite the late hour, the hotel manager was there in person to greet them when the Rolls Royce purred to a stop in front of the Biltmore. The hotel, with its soaring archways and Spanish-colonial detail, had been a mecca for the Hollywood elite since the 1920s when Greta Garbo and Errol Flynn helped put it on the map.

The hotel manager personally escorted them to their suite, the Odell Cottage, the resort's premier accommodation. The luxury cottage, built in 1904, had three bedrooms, a large salon with fireplace, a fireplace in the master bedroom and an exquisite private patio larger than Alexandra's whole house in Culver City.

Bottles of chilled champagne and a stocked refrigerator in the cottage's kitchen came compliments of the hotel. There were plush robes in the marble bathrooms. Any need they had would be met. And then the manager was gone and Alexandra and Wolf were alone.

"I thought he'd never leave," Wolf said, tugging on his white silk bow tie.

Funny how two people could have such different interpretations. Alexandra had wanted the manager never to leave. She wandered through the enormous cottage, thinking only in California would a house this size be called a cottage. The flat beamed ceiling, painted a glossy white, reflected the firelight from the salon's and master bedroom's fireplaces. Votive candles had been lit on the mantel. More candles flickered in the bathroom on the marble ledge beneath the mirror. And then she noticed the dresser in the master bedroom.

Oh, God. She turned away from the dresser groaning beneath the dozens of vivid red, passion-red roses, her stomach heaving up and down as though she were doing jumping jacks. What was she doing here?

"You can't avoid me forever," Wolf drawled from the doorway, startling her. She nervously glanced at him over her shoulder, suddenly feeling as though he were a complete stranger.

In ways he was.

She'd seen him in countless movies, had kissed him and been escorted around town by him, but she didn't know him, didn't know what he really thought about anything, much less her.

"I'm not trying to avoid you," she said defensively, watching him pull his bow tie from around his collar and toss the silk onto the table near the bed. She heard the anxious note in her voice and moved past him to return to the cottage's stylish living room.

The warm fire drew her, and she crouched in her full white bridal gown in front of the hearth, hands outstretched.

"You're running away from me," Wolf said with certainty, turning to watch her.

A lump filled her throat and she curled her fingers against the fire's heat. He wasn't far off the mark. She was scared.

Scared of what would happen next. But she couldn't tell him that she was still as inexperienced as she had been four years ago, that she still didn't know how to pleasure a man or…be pleasured by a man.

Jerkily Alexandra pulled the Italian lace veil from her head and folded it into a neat square before rising. "Why should I avoid you?" she said, keeping her voice even, battling to keep her fear at bay. "This is just a studio stunt, a media ploy that will soon be resolved—"

"No," he interrupted, still standing in the doorway, his coat now off, his shirt partway unbuttoned. "Wrong."

Her heart stuttered. She was glad he was far away, glad he couldn't see how she'd begun to shake. Give her a wild horse and she'd ride it, but give her a man like Wolf…

Alexandra licked her upper lip, her nerves making her mouth dry. During the reception she'd done everything in her power to keep from being alone with him, had done everything she could to pretend she wasn't married to him, but it was awfully hard now that they were here, in the bridal suite, alone.

His dark eyes narrowed fractionally. "As I said while we were dancing, I wouldn't marry just anyone. I certainly wouldn't marry someone for publicity or for my career. I married you because I want you."

Wolf's voice was deep, thick, like honey in sunlight, and it drugged her senses almost as much as his heady, dizzying kisses.

"I want you," he repeated again, quieter, deeper, his voice hypnotic.

Alexandra looked across the room at him and her brain felt slow, thoughts scattered, fuzzy. With Wolf's dark hair falling forward on his brow he looked as wild and untamable as his namesake. "You don't know me. You said so yourself."

He stretched out his hands, the shirt pulling wider, revealing his chest and the bronzed plane of muscle. "Then this is where we start."

He was a man, a beautiful, primitive, masculine man, and the idea that he wanted her, that he desired her, filled her with fear and nerves and curiosity.

He wasn't even touching her, just looking at her, and yet she felt as though he'd already taken her in his arms, run his hands down the length of her. She felt edgy, taut, physical, aware of her skin, her face and lips, her body where it curved, her legs where they joined. She felt all her fingers and toes. The indentation of her waist. The fullness of her hips and breasts.

He made her aware that she was a woman.

But that was the thing—what did a man do with a woman? Oh, she knew the mechanics—how could a farm girl not know?—but the scenes from films, the love scenes and the heat and the passion and the desperation…

And what would a woman do with a man?

Wolf was unbuttoning the rest of his dress shirt now, and she stared at him, watching the way he moved, his hands, the corded muscles of his arms. She watched his eyes, the focus, the intensity, the flare of heat in his dark eyes.

He was waking something in her, stirring her as much as if she'd been on his lap, his hand on her belly, covering her, warming her, making her feel the hunger only he had ever made her feel.

Shirt off, he reached for the button on his trousers. Alexandra's eyes grew wider, her mouth drier. Her heart thumped as she watched him undo the button. "We can't," she finally choked out. "*I* can't."

"Why not?"

"It'd be wrong—"

He started walking toward her. "We're married."

"In a fake ceremony with a fake minister and fake guests!"

"The minister and guests were real," he said mildly, watching her take a step away from the fire, behind the couch, doing her best to avoid him, "which means the ceremony was real, too."

She pressed her hands to the back of the elegant sofa. "But you know this is over as soon as your film wraps."

She felt cornered, caught, as though he'd been a real wolf tracking her. And now he had her where he wanted her to be. A shudder coursed through her, a shudder of fear, a shudder of desire. "This is just temporary," she insisted breathlessly, knowing she couldn't manage him. Or this.

He suddenly moved so fast she didn't have a chance to escape, and he was there at her side, circling her wrists with his hands. "I don't think I ever said that," he said, the pads of his thumbs caressing her frantic pulse.

But I did, she thought, trying to keep from losing her head. "But I did. I do—"

"And the film," he continued, interrupting her, "might never wrap. It's a cursed film, has been from the start." And then he tugged her toward him, one resistant inch at a time until she could feel the heat of his body scorch hers through the silk bodice of her wedding gown.

"You're my wife," he said, tugging her even more firmly, pulling her off balance so that she fell helplessly against him.

She inhaled sharply as his knees parted and she tumbled into his arms, his hips cradling hers, her breasts crushed against his chest. And then his head descended, and his mouth covered hers, stifling her gasp, catching her breath.

She was lost again, she thought, the pressure of his mouth on hers turning her inside out, making her lose track of all thought, all reason.

No wonder all his costars fell so hard for him. He kissed them senseless, kissed them into surrender and submission.

She gripped his shirt, desperate to find some center, some sanity, but his tongue was teasing the inside of her lip and she was shivering, burning from the inside out. Something about his mouth on hers made her want to open herself, open her mouth and body for him.

And the more she wanted him, the more certain she was that this was wrong, these feelings were wrong, and panicked, she now pressed at his chest. She'd intended to push away, but the sinewy planes of his chest felt shockingly good.

His body was warm and hard, his muscle dense and smooth beneath the palm of her hand.

He felt too good. This all felt too good. Anything this good had to be...

Wrong.

"Stop," she choked out against his mouth.

His hand reached up, tangled in her hair. "Why?"

"This is crazy. It doesn't make sense."

She felt his chest lift, fall, as if filled with silent laughter.

"Passion doesn't have to make sense," he answered before drawing her closer again, his hand sliding from her hair, down her back, to rest on her hips. Despite the full skirt she felt him, his strength and hunger, as well as his hand as it curved over her backside, shaping her against him.

And as he pressed her to him, he lifted her skirt, found her thighs encased in silk, and with a snap he unhooked the garter belt from the top of each thigh-high stocking.

With her skirt still lifted, he pulled her back against him, rubbed her hips against his so she could feel him, the hard length of him barely restrained by his thin trousers.

She gasped as her belly clenched tight and heat washed through her, filling her, making her insides feel warm and liquid.

He rubbed her against him again and her breath caught in her throat. His erection was long, hard, thick, and yet when the tip brushed against the apex of her legs, she felt little shock waves rush through her.

Felt muscles she didn't even know she had, start to squeeze.

Felt as though she were melting inside, hot cream, and when he slid his hand beneath her panties her legs wobbled.

No one had ever touched her there, and yet his touch was better than good, his touch made her feel wild, brazen, and she wanted more, wanting him to explore her and soothe all the sensitive nerves that throbbed right now.

"You feel amazing." His voice was deep, passion-rough. "So smooth and soft and slick."

Overwhelmed, she buried her face against his chest, her arms around him, her hands fists in his lower back.

"Wet," he added, his voice a velvet sandpaper on her senses. "You're wet for me."

He was still touching her, lightly, delicately, the curls, the lips, the wildly sensitive hardened nub, and she was wet and growing wetter. And then when he slid a finger inside her, she bucked at his touch, amazed at how much she felt, at the heady sensation of being explored by him.

Her response nearly pushed him over the edge, and he turned her around, tugged and ripped at the back of the dress until the tiny jeweled straps fell from her shoulders and the fitted bodice opened and tumbled forward, revealing her high, round breasts.

"You are beyond beautiful," he said, hands covering her breasts, feeling her nipples stiffen, harden beneath his hands.

Self-control nearly shattered, Wolf stretched her out in front of the fire, and for a moment he just looked at her, rose-tipped breasts bare, skirts tangled around her legs and the glow of the fire warming her skin.

He unzipped his pants as he watched her face. "I want you." His voice was hoarse and his dark eyes burned with barely leashed hunger.

She nodded once, her heart pounding too hard for her to actually answer.

His sculptured features were taut. His eyes smoldered. Again he struck her as fire and ice, ancient Celtic myth twined with a thousand years of Spanish passion.

Alexandra felt a stirring inside her, a whisper in her heart, something infinitely special and rare, something magical that not everyone might know.

She loved him.

Emotion surged through her, fierce and unexpected. She wanted this man, she wanted him completely.

"I don't know how to do this," she said as he moved between her legs, his erection pressing urgently between her thighs, the tip of his shaft silky against her dampness.

He'd started to enter her, but now he stopped. He'd felt the resistance inside her, too. His weight on his forearms, he looked down at her, searched her eyes. "You've never—"

"No," she whispered, aware of his stomach and hips and thighs covering hers. It was so intimate and dominant she shook, her thighs quivering from tension.

"I'm the first?" he asked.

The tears weren't far off, but they weren't tears of fear. They were pure emotion.

It was so surreal being here like this, married to Wolf, making love for the first time as his bride. His *wife.* "Yes," she answered huskily.

He kissed her deeply.

"I don't want to hurt you," he murmured against her mouth even as she felt the heat of his body throb inside her. He hadn't broken her hymen yet. He was uncertain, too, she realized. He was afraid of giving her pain.

Her eyes burned hotter. His body felt like lava inside her. But it was nothing compared to the tenderness in her heart. Wolf would be her first lover, and if fate was good, hopefully her last.

He stroked the side of her face, wiping away the one tear trickling over her cheekbone. "You're crying."

"It's a big night."

"It is," he agreed and he'd never sounded more Irish.

His dark eyes met hers and held, and there was suddenly no mask, no wall up between them, nothing but a beautiful fire in his eyes, a passion and hunger that spoke of dreams unfulfilled and hope he still cherished. Wolf might be the world's most beloved star, but he was also a man still searching for love. And a home.

"Take me," she said, sliding her hands down his back to his narrow hips, hard with sinewy muscle. "Don't be afraid. I'm not."

And then he was kissing her again, kissing her as if she were the last woman on earth and this the last kiss ever. He pressed forward as he kissed her, pressing against the resistance, and then she felt him, full and hard, filling her, deeper and deeper still.

It did hurt, but at the same time it was wondrous, new, sacred. Sacred because it felt right. Sacred because somehow she knew she'd always been waiting for him. Even that one painful night four years ago had just been a detour until they finally got to where they were supposed to go.

Here.

Right here, together, like this.

His hips rocked, thrusting into her, and she felt the hot fire start to give way to a different sensation, one of warmth and fullness and even pleasure.

As he stroked her, moving in and out, she instinctively squeezed down on him, savoring his hardness, his strength, the feel of him taking her, making her his in front of the fire while she still wore her wedding gown, the full skirts and stiff petticoat ruched around her hips, the garter belt around her waist, the white silk stockings rolled down to her knees.

When his tempo increased, the pleasure did, too. Her hands slid across his back and she whimpered at the building tension, the way everything was tightening, turning, both maddening and exciting.

She'd been shy before they made love, but now that they were here, like this, in this together, she wanted whatever it was he could give her. She wanted all of what this could be, all of what they could be.

As the tension built, Alexandra felt more frantic, her hips rising to meet his, pressing against him.

"You can come," he whispered against her throat, his lips warm, his teeth nipping at the column of her neck. "Let go. Come for me."

And then as he drove into her harder, faster, pushing her ever closer to that point of no return, she was suddenly, spectacularly there, exploding in waves of intense pleasure, the rhythmic contractions electric blue and silver shock waves that rippled through her one after another. The pleasure was unlike anything she'd known before, and her body still shuddered with exquisite sensitivity when Wolf came, too, pumping even deeper into her, and as he filled her body, he filled her heart.

I love him, she thought, wrapping her arms around his neck and pressing her face to his shoulder. *I love this man.*

CHAPTER TEN

SHE WAS STILL WRAPPED in Wolf's arms, her body not yet cool, when he lifted his head, kissed her once and then pulled away.

Standing, he gazed down at her where she lay half-naked in her crumpled, stained bridal gown, her pale breasts bare, the white skirts hiked high around her hips. "Yet another ruined gown," he said.

He was referring to her vintage Armani gown, and she smiled faintly. "I don't mind this time."

"I should have undressed you completely."

She tucked a tendril of hair back, away from her eyes. "I'm glad you didn't. It was more exciting this way."

"You are a Hollywood girl after all," he said, scooping her into his arms and carrying her into the bathroom, where he stripped her and walked her into the shower with him.

He lathered her beneath the steaming shower spray, rubbing the suds across her breasts, down over her stomach, her hips, her bottom and then gently between her tender thighs. "Sore?" he asked as, shivering with pleasure, she leaned against him.

If she thought about it, she was sore, but it wasn't bad, not like the terrible violation she'd feared. In fact, making love with Wolf had made her body feel better, made *her* feel better. Made her feel…complete, although she wasn't sure how that worked.

"I'm good," she murmured as he bathed her with the handheld shower head, washing the bubbles from her now pink

breasts and then lower to rinse the suds from the cleft in her
bottom and her bottom itself.

She gasped as he continued to rinse her from behind, the
jetted spray caressing the backs of her thighs and then between.
He'd angled the showerhead so that the tingling spray struck
her sensitive folds and the small peaked nub at the top of her
inner lips.

She clutched at his arm, torn between pleasure and shame.

"Does this hurt?" he asked, his voice passion-rough.

"No." She blushed. "I'm just…shy."

"Close your eyes then."

She was beginning to pant at the erotic beating of water on
her tender skin. "Is this right?"

"There's nothing wrong with me giving you pleasure," he
said, gently widening her legs with his knee and bringing the
showerhead closer to her. "You're mine now and I want you to
feel good."

Her legs quivered beneath her, and she clung to Wolf's arm,
her hand wrapped around his tight bicep as the warm water
teased her, tormented her, bringing her closer to another orgasm.

"Wolf," she choked out, the heat inside her building, rising.
"I don't want…I can't…come—"

"Don't worry, love. You can come. You won't be alone."

And, opening her eyes, she looked down. While he was
pleasuring her with the showerhead in his right hand, he was
stroking himself with his left.

Pulse racing, senses enflamed, she felt the warm water
caress her even as she watched Wolf stroke his erection.

His shaft was huge, hard, the head a perfect smooth cap
tinged with pink, and as his hand rode the length, she felt
overcome not by shyness but wonder. He was beautiful, the way
he was made was beautiful, and as he stroked himself, the
muscles in his abdomen knotted and his bicep clenched.

She heard him groan, a deep, guttural groan, and it was
primitive and raw and the sexiest thing she'd ever heard.

He was close to coming, and that's when Alexandra stopped
fighting her orgasm, opening her legs just a little wider, rocking

forward on her toes so the water pressure was right where she wanted it most. And then she was there, a gasp, a muffled cry, and then with a louder cry she climaxed with him.

A few minutes later, dry and wrapped in the hotel's plush robe, a rosy-cheeked Alexandra joined Wolf in raiding the cottage's stocked refrigerator.

Famished, they sampled the platter of cheese and crackers, then Wolf fed Alexandra bites of chocolate-covered strawberries between fizzy sips of delicate gold champagne.

Finally they found their way into the bedroom and, with robes discarded, lay close together beneath the fluffiest feather duvet Alexandra had ever encountered.

The wedding had been terrifying. The reception overwhelming. And the lovemaking mind-blowing.

She smiled into the crook of her arm and blushed remembering everything she and Wolf had just done.

My God, he did it for her. In every way. And finally, finally all the questions about sex had been answered and her curiosity put to rest.

Making love with Wolf was better than anything she'd ever imagined, and waiting to make love with him was worth all the sleepless nights, the impossible fantasies, the sharp, relentless craving she'd felt when he touched her, kissed her, aroused the dormant fire in her.

Snuggling close to him, she felt his arm wrap more snugly around her and pull her back until her bottom rested against his hips and his hand covered her breast. Even though she was exhausted, she felt a flare of heat all over again, desire licking at her, through her, tightening her nipples until they pebbled beneath Wolf's hand.

He laughed softly behind her, his breath tickling the back of her neck. "Go to sleep," he said, his voice vibrating through her, low, husky, sexy. Amused. "Or you'll be too sore to enjoy it again tomorrow."

They did make love again in the morning, a slow, sensual coming together that made Alexandra feel utterly fulfilled and extremely lazy. But the warm, languid mood evaporated as soon as Wolf told her the plans for the rest of the day.

"We're leaving for Africa this afternoon?" She rolled away and sat up, clutching the duvet to her chest. "On the first day of our honeymoon?"

"You knew we were going—"

"I knew *you* were going." She sat back, wrapped the covers around her, leaving Wolf naked. But that was fine—he didn't have a modest bone in his body. "And I didn't think you were going until tomorrow."

He shrugged and left the bed. "There must have been some miscommunication."

She sat there watching as he headed for the shower. *"Wolf."*

He reached into the glass shower, turned the handles, adjusted the water's temperature. "You've known all along I'm going on location," he said before climbing in.

That was one way of ending a discussion, she thought irritably, waiting for him to finish. And when she heard the water turn off, she was at the shower door, waiting for him to step out.

"Yes, I know *you* need to go away," she said, resuming the discussion where they'd left off, "but we never discussed me going with you."

He rubbed the white towel over his wet hair and face before mopping his chest and wrapping the towel snugly around his lean hips. "If you weren't joining me, Alexandra, why did we have you apply for a passport?" When she didn't answer, he shrugged and reached for his shave cream and razor. "Hop into the shower. It's a British Airways flight this afternoon. We can't be late."

One second they were still on the runway in Los Angeles and the next they were off.

Zambia. Africa.

Alex curled her fingers into her palm, hiding the sudden tremor in her veins. She knew Wolf's next picture—an adaptation of the novel *The Burning Shore*—was to be filmed there, but she'd never been to Africa, had never been to

Europe. And except for trips into neighboring Canada with her family when she was a little girl, she'd never been out of the United States.

It was a long flight but comfortable, as they were flying first class on British Airways and everyone on board, from the captain to the purser to the newest wide-eyed flight attendant, personally welcomed Wolf on board.

After the five-course dinner, the wide leather seats actually turned into flat, surprisingly comfortable beds.

Alexandra woke to breakfast, coffee and news that they'd be landing in a little over two hours.

But by the time they arrived in Lusaka, Zambia's biggest city as well as airport, Alexandra was ready to stretch her legs and move around.

Unfortunately their journey wasn't over yet, as the plane that had been chartered to ferry Wolf and Alexandra to the set wasn't at the airport. Wolf made a few calls and put the alternatives before Alexandra: they could either overnight in Lusaka and hope the plane would be available tomorrow or hire one of the safari services to drive them to the lodge in Kafue National Park.

Alexandra opted for hiring a driver. It was only a four hour drive and she'd had enough flying for one day.

She'd seen plenty of Land Rovers in Los Angeles—the celebrity crowd liked driving them—but as their cases were transferred into the roofless four-by-four vehicle, she realized that Land Rovers in Africa were actually utilitarian jeeps.

The driver, a safari guide who'd once been a poacher before serving time behind bars, was now an ardent conservationist and eager to share his love for Zambia's country and culture.

Kafue, he told them, was Zambia's oldest park and the largest. Established in 1950, it was the second largest national park in the world and about the size of Wales.

Their lodge and encampment was situated on the banks of the Kafue River in the Namwala West area.

The farther they traveled from Lusaka and the highway, the more primitive conditions got, with the road sometimes disappearing for miles at a time. Alexandra clung to a handrail on the side of the Land Rover as the blue-gray vehicle bumped and shuddered over the grassy, rocky and pothole-scarred terrain.

Some of the bumps were small and others were bone-jarring. As a small airplane flew overhead, Alexandra glanced up, wishing now they'd maybe waited for the charter flight. That had to be easier on the joints than this.

By late afternoon they were traveling through the brachystegia woodland broken by fantastically shaped kopjes. The scenery was spectacular, the colors of the landscape every shade of green and gold. They passed enormous herds of impala and hartebeest and then later a herd of puku grazing with zebra while a lone puku buck stood off to the side, head up, alert, on guard to protect the others.

"Are there big game animals here?" Alexandra asked as flocks of colorful birds lifted from a nearby tree.

"Lions, leopards, cheetahs, elephants," he counted on his fingers. "Hippo at the river, and where you're staying there are quite a few."

Alexandra glanced excitedly at Wolf. "We're on the river?"

"Your lodge has a deck overhanging the riverbanks. At twilight you'll see many of the animals come to drink."

And then suddenly they were there, on the banks of the deep blue Kafue River. The lodge stood two stories tall, dominating the camp with its steep thatched roof and pale-yellow-pigmented mud-and-plaster walls.

A dozen smaller thatched bungalows bordered the wide river. Those, Alexandra discovered, were reserved for the principal actors, directors and senior production staff, while the rest of the film crew would be billeted in the dozen new tent cabins just recently pitched.

As Tom and Alice Stewart, owners of the Kafue Lodge, came out to greet Wolf, they spotted their Zambian driver, a man who over the years had become a great friend. As everyone talked and caught up on news, Alexandra walked along the wooden deck toward the river to stretch her legs and get her bearings.

Africa.

Africa. Zambia. Kafue. Silently she repeated the exotic

names as she faced the river, basking in the sun as the late, long rays of light painted the opposite riverbank copper and jade.

"Sorry you came?" Wolf asked, standing a little ways behind her.

She wasn't entirely surprised to hear his voice. She'd felt him near, watching her, protecting her.

"No." She turned, smiled at him over her shoulder. "This is amazing. We're honeymooning in Africa."

He walked toward her, hands in his pockets, his handsome jaw shadowed with a day's growth of beard. "I've always loved Africa. It's why I wanted to do this movie. It was a chance to bring the country I love to the screen."

He was gazing out across the river, eyes narrowed, dense black lashes fanning his high cheekbones, and Alexandra flashed to their wedding night and the wonderful and wicked things they'd done together.

Biting her lip, she fought to suppress the flush already creeping up her cheeks.

Wolf caught the blush anyway. "You're not thinking about Africa."

Her blush deepened, her cheeks now scarlet. "No."

"Penny for your thoughts?"

"Oh, no."

He reached out, caught her by the back of her neck, pulled her against him. "That's okay," he murmured mockingly, dark eyes drinking her in. "I know what you're thinking and I want it, too."

And then he was kissing her, turning her world upside down with that dizzying, maddening, knee-melting kiss of his. Her hands crept up to clasp his shirt and then she wound one arm higher, to wrap around his neck. She felt desperate—starved and parched, as though she couldn't get enough.

She couldn't get enough.

It was Wolf who finally ended the kiss, and lifting his head, his black eyebrows rose. "I don't think you're as sweet as your brothers think."

Her lips parted to protest indignantly, but instead she

laughed, a great big belly laugh that had tears smarting her eyes. "I think you're finally starting to get to know me."

Wolf was being hailed by one of the film crew standing at the lodge, but he didn't immediately go. Instead he stroked her cheek with his thumb. "There's a lot more I'd like to know, too. And that discovery, love, will continue tonight."

Wolf didn't forget his promise either. That evening after a rowdy dinner with the crew that had assembled—Joy, Alexandra noticed, hadn't yet arrived—she found herself relaxing with the predominantly male crew. Having grown up in an all-male household, she was comfortable with men, knew how they talked, understood that they didn't share feelings.

During dinner she good-naturedly endured the teasing, taunts and challenges thrown Wolf's way. As a brand-new husband, the cast and crew were lamenting the end of Wolf's freedom along with his bachelor days.

Wolf was the one who grew weary of the jests. As the moon rose higher in the sky and the crew started in on yet another round of beer and wine, Wolf told Alexandra that they were leaving and calling it a night. "Bring your glass," he said, indicating her empty wine goblet.

"Where are we going?" she asked.

"Back to our room. I've had enough of these blokes. I'd rather be alone with you."

He picked up a bottle of wine and a glass, and with her hand tucked into his they walked away from the lodge and down the flattened grass path to their *rondavel*.

Inside, he set the wine on the nightstand, taking her glass from her and placing it beside the bottle. But once Wolf took Alexandra into his arms, his mouth covering hers and turning her into a slave of her own senses, the wine was forgotten.

Joy didn't arrive the next day either, causing considerable consternation in camp. Alexandra noticed the director and key staff engaging in several serious conversations at the open-air *boma* that overlooked the bend in the river. It was early spring and the tropical climate was temperate, with mornings and evenings decidedly cool while midday was sunny and extremely pleasant. However, the rainy season was just six weeks away and every day on location was precious. They couldn't afford wasted days and yet there was little they could do without Joy, as she was in virtually every scene in the movie.

Late afternoon Daniel called for a read-through of the script and asked Alexandra if she'd mind reading Joy's lines to allow the rest of the cast a chance to go through the script together.

She was embarrassed at first, but Daniel insisted, and as Alexandra took a seat at the long table in the lodge, Wolf gave her an encouraging nod. After a while she was so engrossed in the plot and story she lost her self-consciousness and enjoyed the read-through.

It was nearly dinner by the time they finished. Alice appeared as they were ending the read-through to invite everyone to the river *boma* for appetizers and cocktails.

"We've a bartender pouring drinks," she said. "And if you're lucky, you'll see some of our famous wildlife—and no, I'm not just talking about my husband Tom."

Wolf waited for Alexandra while she returned Joy's script to Daniel and together they headed for the river bar. The sun was setting on the horizon, and as the deep lavender shadows stretched along the river, game began to appear.

Standing on the elevated rosewood deck, Wolf drew her in front of him and wrapped his arm around her shoulders. He felt so good, so warm and strong and solid. She reached up, covered his forearm with her hands, held him to her. She felt so safe standing together like this, absolutely secure. If only she could always feel this way.

Folding chairs covered in zebra and gemsbok dotted the deck and gradually they filled with the cast and crew. In the distance a lion roared, and Alexandra jumped, still not used to having real lions so close. Last night she'd woken to use the en suite bathroom and a deep huffing sound outside their *rondavel* had scared her—enough to wake Wolf as she'd scampered back into bed. Turned out the huffing had been a lioness walking through camp, trying to attract the attention of her mate.

Alexandra ended up getting the attention of her mate, too.

Wolf must have remembered last night's middle-of-the-night seduction because he suddenly bent his head and nipped at the side of her neck, hardening her nipples and sending goose bumps up and down her arms.

"Not here," she whispered, voice husky.

"Then let's have a drink and excuse ourselves," he said even as he slipped a hand between them to caress her backside.

It was getting hotter and harder to breathe, and as much as Alexandra liked the film crew, she didn't think making love in front of them was such a good idea. Taking a quick step, she broke out of his arms. "Wait there. I'll get the drinks."

"You have two minutes or I'm dragging you back to the bungalow minus refreshments."

She laughed, wagged her finger reprovingly at him. "We can't go to our bungalow yet. Everyone will talk. We should at least wait until after dinner."

"I can't wait."

"Yes you can."

His dark eyes flashed a warning. "Fine. I'll just make you pay later."

She laughed again because when Wolf was like this he made her feel good, reminding her of the days at home when she used to challenge her brothers. She didn't used to be afraid of anything.

As Alexandra waited her turn in line, she looked out at the river, now growing murky as dusk gave way to night. She liked it here in the "bush," as their hosts Tom and Alice called it. She liked the smell, the feel, the pattern of the days.

Life was very communal, with everyone coming together at the lodge for meals, but then once the sun went down, the fire pit became the hub of social activity.

In the evenings the fireplace was surrounded by folding canvas chairs where the guests—in this case the crew and cast—relaxed, sipping cold vodkas, drinking beer and exchanging stories late into the night.

Being in camp at Kafue was almost like being in Montana on the ranch.

Just then a lion growled, louder, closer, and Alexandra shivered and grinned. Well, *almost* like Montana. Not quite.

During dinner Daniel deVoors drew Wolf into a discussion with the lighting director about setting up the cameras for the first scene they wanted to shoot. The lighting director had been watching the way the sun moved through the sky the past few days and the quality of light.

Alexandra leaned back in her chair and listened without really paying attention. The truth was she only had eyes for Wolf.

Spanish-Irish Wolf Kerrick with his savage beauty. Dark-haired, dark-eyed, with soul and sin carved into his features.

He knew the effect he had on women, she thought, knew how he could lay waste to an entire continent with a lift of a brow, the curve of his lip.

He'd possessed her imagination the very same way. She hadn't wanted to want him, had been sure this time she could, she would, resist him.

She'd been wrong.

As if he could feel her long scrutiny, Wolf turned his head, looked at her, meeting her gaze. Their eyes locked, held.

Desire flared, hot and tangible.

Abruptly Wolf pushed back his chair, murmured something unintelligible to the others, but before he could completely break away, a laughing female voice called to them in the darkness.

"Now did you all really think I wasn't coming?"

Alexandra froze, heart still thumping even though the blood began to chill in her veins.

Joy Hughes had just arrived.

CHAPTER ELEVEN

WHERE WAS HE?

Wolf still hadn't come to bed yet and now it was after midnight.

Alexandra had spent the past three hours waiting for him, two and a half of those hours in bed. Two and a half hours where every minute felt endless, where she jumped at every creak outside, where she waited nervously, anxiously, stomach churning, imagination worked overtime.

Where was he? What was he doing? Who was he with?

Some questions were more easily answered than others. She knew he was here in the camp. A sixth sense told her Wolf was with Joy. And as to what they were doing, Alexandra didn't even want to imagine that...

If only he'd return. Or if she could only fall asleep and escape her crazy, punishing thoughts.

Instead she lay restless in the big bed beneath the thatched roof with the white gauzy mosquito netting draped around the mattress.

Why *had* Wolf married her? Why had he thought it necessary to go through with the wedding? Was it really about the lethal cocktail she'd ingested and the fallout of publicity and her family's outrage? Or was the wedding an attempt to cover something else?

To cover for someone else?

A stunt to distract everyone from what was really happening...

What *was* really happening?

Tears stung her eyes. She rolled over onto her stomach, pressed her face into her pillow, hoping to make the tears stop.

Alexandra woke much later to the mattress sagging beneath Wolf's weight as he slid into bed. Her heart thumped as she felt him adjust the covers. She wondered if he'd reach for her, hold her or even say something. But he didn't come near her. And lying there in the dark, she listened as he sighed a deep gut-wrenching sigh. The sound was so heavy, so sorrowful that Alexandra's heart fell, tumbling all the way down.

Now that Joy had arrived, nothing was going to be the same.

The next morning the cast sat down with Daniel for a second read-through. Daniel again asked Alexandra to join them, not to read anyone's lines this time but to listen and learn. "You're the one who wants to be a director," he said, offering her a chair to his left.

Wolf was already seated at the table, four chairs down from Daniel. When Joy arrived with her cup of hot tea, she grabbed a chair next to Wolf, sliding in with a conspiratorial wink.

"You've already done a read-through," Joy said, getting comfortable before lifting and blowing on her tea. "But who played me?"

It was quiet for a moment and then Wolf answered, "Alex did."

Joy took a tiny sip of her tea, her dark-winged eyebrows arching higher. "Alex who?"

There was another odd moment of silence as various cast members glanced at Wolf and Alexandra. Wolf cleared his throat, gestured to Alex, who was sitting with Daniel. "Alexandra. My wife."

Joy hesitated ever so slightly and then laughed, a light tinkling laugh to fill the strained silence. But she never once looked at Alex or acknowledged her directly. "That's right. You're married now. I forgot. Silly me."

Alexandra stared at Joy for a long moment, even as one of the vervet monkeys who'd decided to make Kafue Lodge home tossed pieces of grass down on the table. Alexandra seethed on the inside. How could Joy have forgotten that Wolf was married?

Or did Joy just intend to pretend that Wolf was still single? That everything between them was still the same?

Temper boiling, Alexandra leaned forward. "Did your husband come with you, Joy?"

Joy looked almost startled by Alexandra's question, and Wolf looked furious.

Joy forced a tight smile, shook her head. "No."

Daniel intervened at that moment, crisply directing everyone to open their scripts to the first scene, and Alexandra opened her notebook but not before she saw the look Wolf was giving her. He looked stunned. And furious. There was, Alexandra thought shakily, her bravado giving way, going to be hell to pay later.

She was right. As everyone took a break for lunch, Wolf immediately made a beeline for Alexandra. "Let's take a walk," he said tersely."

She'd been standing next to Daniel at the time, and the director gave her an apologetic look before disappearing.

"I don't feel like a walk right now," she answered, trying to hang on to her anger, trying to find the courage she'd felt earlier. Wolf was her husband. She had a right to stand up for herself. She had a right to tell other women to back off, too, especially if the other woman happened to be Wolf's former lover.

"It's not really an option." Wolf's tone was clipped, grim. "We need to talk."

What Wolf really meant was that he needed to talk and Alexandra needed to listen. As they crossed from the lodge, the raised wood deck gave way to a dirt path, and they followed the path a short distance along the river while the peering eyes of half-submerged hippos followed them.

"What was that back there?" Wolf demanded, stopping beneath one of the many large evergreen waterberry trees shadowing the riverbank.

Alexandra knew she couldn't feign ignorance. She knew why he was upset, but maybe it was time he discovered how she felt. "You insisted we get married, Wolf. You said you had a responsibility to me."

Monkeys chattered above them in the tree, dropping bits of leaves and fruit stems on their heads.

"I'm perfectly aware of my responsibilities."

"Then why do I feel like you'd rather be Joy's husband than mine?"

"Don't be absurd."

"I'm not." Her voice throbbed with outrage. "You're the one that didn't come to bed last night until two in the morning—"

"You were awake?"

"I waited for you."

He sighed impatiently, brushed a stem off his shoulder. "Alexandra, you know Joy's a close friend of mine. She'd just arrived in camp. It's a long trip here, she'd had a series of misadventures—"

"Then she should bring her own husband, not use mine!"

Wolf took a step back, jaw dropping. He lifted a hand to his mouth, giving her a look that wasn't hard to decipher. He thought she was childish, beyond childish. He loathed her right now. "Don't be petty or unkind," he said quietly. "It doesn't suit you."

Then he turned and walked off, heading back to the lodge.

Everyone was eating lunch outside, scattered around the cold fire pit or on the deck with views of the river. Tom had pointed out the family of crocodiles sunning themselves on the opposite side of the river, and everyone passed binoculars as they ate the African barbecue lunch of *borewors*—grilled sausages.

Alexandra ate with a couple of the lighting technicians since Wolf was deep in discussion with Daniel and Joy. He didn't look at her once during lunch, and his cool dismissal stung.

After lunch everyone returned to meetings and Alexandra pulled a book from her carry-on travel bag and found a chair at the deserted *boma* at the river.

She was still sitting there two hours later when Daniel deVoors appeared. He hadn't shaved in days and the gold-brown bristles on his face glinted in the sunlight. "Beautiful here, isn't it?" he commented.

She nodded, put down her book. "I love it. Reminds me of Montana."

He laughed, pulled up a chair. "Reminds me of South Africa. I grew up there until I was sixteen and then my family moved to Australia and then the States." He dragged another chair toward them, put his feet on the seat. "Wolf is a total beast today. What's going on?"

Daniel had been there at the very beginning. He and Benjamin had helped set up the meeting with Wolf. "We got in a fight," she said lowly. "About Joy."

"Joy's beautiful."

Alexandra nodded. "I guess I'm jealous."

Daniel cocked his head. "Wolf married you."

"Because Joy was already married."

"What does Wolf say?"

"That I'm being petty."

"What do you think?"

She looked up at him, expression serious. "I think she's a threat. I think Wolf still has feelings for her."

"And I think Wolf always will. Wolf's the most loyal person I know. He takes care of his friends."

She made a rough sound, hating the rush of emotion. "So what do I do?"

"Be nice to Joy?"

She said nothing, and after a moment Daniel leaned forward, patted her knee. "If they really wanted to be together, they'd be together, Alexandra. It's easy to get a divorce." He gave her an encouraging smile. "Chin up and don't let things you can't control get you down."

She and Wolf still weren't speaking as they both washed and dressed for dinner—which meant Wolf put on a clean shirt and she added a sweater over her knit top.

Outside, around the fire, Alexandra's spirits continued to sink. Wolf was sitting near her, but he could have been anyone as he didn't acknowledge her.

Alexandra had never felt like such an outsider. Or a failure.

Four years in Los Angeles. Four years and now this.

She'd moved to Los Angeles with high hopes. She'd wanted to succeed, she'd wanted to be respected, she'd wanted to be important. *Valued.* And playing Wolf's love interest and then marrying him had gotten her recognition but not respect.

Certainly not self-respect.

Hyenas laughed hysterically in the dark and Alexandra crossed her arms over her chest, suppressing a shiver, thinking the hyenas tonight could be laughing at her.

They should be laughing at her.

Alexandra had wanted to prove herself, had wanted to show her family that she was smart, independent, savvy. Instead she'd discovered she was just as naive as they'd feared. Instead of succeeding on her own merit, she'd made a name for herself dating a famous actor.

Marrying a famous actor.

She glanced at Wolf and realized with a jolt he was looking at her. His dark eyes were shuttered. She couldn't tell what he was thinking, but she wondered if tonight he was as full of regrets as she was.

Wolf brusquely stood. "I'm going to bed," he announced, saying good-night to everyone. "See you tomorrow."

Alexandra watched him turn to leave, again without speaking to her, filling her with hurt and then indignation. Was he just going to ignore her forever?

And while he ignored her, what did he expect her to do? They were camped in the middle of the African bush. The next safari lodge was a two-hour drive away. She had no one but him and the crew to talk to.

Although Alexandra dreaded being confrontational, she jumped up from her chair and went after Wolf.

"This isn't working," she said, following Wolf's steps as he climbed the stairs to their elevated *rondavel.*

"No," he agreed, pivoting on the deck, "it's not."

"So what happens now?" she asked. "Do I go home? Do we get a divorce—"

"A divorce?" he interrupted incredulously, his profile bathed in moonlight. "I'm Irish-Spanish."

"So?"

"I don't believe in divorce and I won't accept that as a satisfactory solution."

Silence stretched and Alexandra wasn't sure where to look, what to do. She could hear a splash in the river and wondered if it was a hippo or a crocodile, wondered if the old male hippo that Tom had nicknamed Alfred would come foraging through camp tonight as he had last night.

Sighing, she pushed back a thick handful of hair from her face. "You know, you're not the kind of man I ever planned to settle down with."

"No?"

She shook her head slowly. "No."

"Why not?"

"I guess I wanted someone like my dad. He loved my mom so much." Alexandra's voice suddenly thickened with emotion. "She was diagnosed with cancer when I was four, and my dad fought for her with everything he had. He was not going to lose her." Blinking, she prayed he wouldn't see her tears. "And that's what I wanted when I grew up. A man who'd fight for me."

"And that's why you were still a virgin at twenty-three? You were holding out for a hero?"

She hated his mocking tone, hated that he'd laugh at her when she was sharing something so deeply personal, so incredibly painful. Anger rushed through her and she clamped her jaw tight.

The river and surrounding reserve were alive with wildlife tonight. In the distance a lion growled, and much closer monkeys shrieked in the cluster of palm and waterberry trees lining the river.

"Not a hero," she said finally, breaking the silence, "but a man who has grown up. A man who knows what's important. A man who'd honor his commitment to me."

Wolf didn't answer and Alexandra turned to look at him. He was leaning on the deck rail, watching her, his face partially shadowed.

His silence unnerved her. His silence made her feel small and ridiculous and insignificant all over again. Steeling herself,

Alex forced a cool, careless smile. "You think I'm childish and immature. Overly sensitive and too emotional, right?"

Again he didn't answer. Not immediately. Then he shook his head. "No," he said quietly. "I don't."

Her heart thumped painfully hard, and she waited, hoping he'd say more, hoping he'd explain himself, his actions and silences, his irritation and distance, but he didn't.

If only she understood him better. If only she knew what motivated him and what was important to him and why.

"It's late," he said, pushing off the rail. "I'm tired, going to bed—"

"Wolf?"

"Yes?"

She searched his face, trying to see something that would help her, trying to learn what she needed to learn. "What kind of woman would you marry?"

He groaned. "Oh, Alexandra."

Shame burned her cheeks, and before she could defend herself he shook his head and added, "The woman I did."

For a moment she didn't understand and she stared at him, confused as well as shy.

"Alexandra, you're the woman I wanted to marry." He reached for her, pulled her to him. "So I did."

He made love to her with an almost ferocious passion, his hunger driven as much by emotion as it was by physical desire. Pinning her arms down above her head, his hands gripped around her wrists, he took her, claiming her, surging into her with fierce, deep thrusts. Alexandra welcomed the intensity, needing the intensity, needing an outlet for her own tangled feelings. But just before she came, he released her wrists and his hands slid over hers, palm to palm, fingers linking.

And, hands locked tightly, head dipped, mouth covering hers, he pushed her to the pinnacle of pleasure and didn't stop, even when she started climaxing. Kissing her, he sucked on her tongue while she exploded around him, her body rippling with pleasure as she held him deep and tight inside her.

The sex was unbelievable, she thought sleepily, curled in his arms afterward, but great sex wasn't going to be enough. She needed his heart.

She needed all of it.

Alexandra woke alone, and as she rolled over inside the mosquito-net tent, she winced at the bright sunlight flooding the *rondavel*. Wolf or one of the housekeepers had opened the wood shutters.

Alexandra hadn't been wearing a watch since it had seemed rather pointless here in the bush, so after taking a fast shower—very fast, as all the hot water was already gone—she dressed in cargo pants and a blue-gray T-shirt and went in search of coffee.

The cast and crew were all busy packing up the Land Rovers and checking the big four-by-four truck that held the cameras. Several Zambian bush guides were on hand this morning to get them to the location they wanted to film as well as to keep an eye out for potential dangers.

Like elephants, Alexandra silently noted. Black rhinos. Lions. Leopards. Cheetahs. Warthogs. And those were just a few, she concluded, taking a sip of the strong, hot coffee she'd sweetened with a smidge of the tinned sweetened condensed milk they used here and another liberal teaspoon of sugar.

And while she savored her coffee, she began to hear bits and pieces of a conversation taking place around the lodge's corner.

"I thought I was going."

It was Joy, Alexandra realized, and she was far from happy.

"I will take you sometime, but you're needed here."

"But, Wolf, you can't go alone. Why don't you wait until I can go with you?"

Stiffening, Alexandra held the hot cup to her lips but didn't drink.

"I'm not going alone," he answered. "Alexandra's going with me."

"But she can't fly and I can! I've always been your copilot. Wait a few days and I'll have a break from shooting and we can go together."

Joy paused and Alexandra had to strain to hear Joy's next

words. "Besides, Wolf, you don't even know *if* she'll go. She might be terrified of small planes, and face it, that little Piper Tri-Pacer isn't the prettiest of aircraft."

"It flies," Wolf said.

"On a wing and a prayer," Joy retorted with a laugh.

Wolf said something in reply that Alexandra didn't catch as Wolf and Joy had begun walking again, heading away from the lodge to the Land Rovers and trucks.

Alexandra was still trying to sort out the meaning of the conversation she'd overheard when Wolf appeared, alone.

"Good morning," he said, bending over to drop a kiss on her lips. And even though his lips just brushed hers, her insides jumped as though she'd been given an electric shock.

"Morning," she answered huskily, making herself take a sip from her cup. "How are you?"

"Good." He dropped into a chair next to hers and propped one boot on top of the other. "I slept great." He looked at her, grinned lazily, teeth flashing. "And you?"

"Good." She took another quick sip, looking at him from beneath lowered lashes. He'd shaved this morning and his hair was thick and glossy black, reflecting the morning sun.

Wolf was studying her just as carefully. "I've got an errand to run today. Feel like coming along?"

This is what Wolf and Joy had been discussing. And Wolf's errand included flying, with Wolf at the controls.

Alexandra wasn't afraid of flying. Three of her five brothers were pilots and they had an airstrip at the Lazy L ranch so her brothers could fly in and out, avoiding the lengthy trip into Bozeman for short hops. But her brothers were expert pilots and their aircraft were always new and scrupulously maintained.

God only knew the maintenance history of the Piper Joy had mentioned.

But then there was Joy, and she'd wanted to make this trip with Wolf and suggested that Alexandra wouldn't want to go and might be afraid to fly. Alexandra was competitive enough not to let Joy win or, in this case, be right.

"I'd love to go," she said cheerfully.

"We're flying."

"Great."

If he questioned her enthusiasm, he gave no indication. "I'll be flying us."

"You're the pilot," she agreed.

One of his eyebrows lifted ever so slightly. "It's a Piper Tri-Pacer."

"A two-seater?"

"Four."

She swallowed around the lump filling her throat. She didn't even know what a Piper Tri-Pacer was. "Let's do it."

He turned his head, looked at her hard. "No questions? Concerns? You're not worried?"

Not worried? She was panicking like mad. Wolf was smart, gorgeous, and while he was amazing in bed, she wasn't sure about his skills as a pilot. And they were flying in a dilapidated plane over the African bush. "My brothers fly," she said airily. "I'm used to little planes."

"Great." Wolf gave her an approving smile. "Let's grab the picnic lunch the kitchen packed and head on out. Big Red's waiting."

"Big Red?"

"The Tri-Pacer."

"Right."

Wrong, Alexandra thought ten minutes later as she stood in front of the saddest excuse for a plane she ever saw.

What must have once been a jaunty red-and-white paint job was now old, chipped, scarred, peeling and faded. The nose looked dinged, the propeller as though it'd tangled with a wildebeest, the tail as if it'd housed a family of baboons. And later Alexandra discovered it had.

On her toes, she peered into the interior, which was nearly all red. Cracked red leather seats with bits of hard yellow foam protruding.

"That's the original leather," Wolf said, tossing their lunch and a huge knapsack into the back of the plane.

As if she hadn't noticed. "Mmm."

"Great little plane."

She stared at the red cockpit with its black instrument panels, the radio and the headphones dangling from the yoke. It was definitely snug inside. And while Wolf had called it a four-seater, she couldn't imagine squeezing two people in the very cramped backseat.

Belted in next to Wolf, she saw him wave to Tom, who'd come down to the primitive airstrip to see them off.

"We'll be back before dark," Wolf shouted.

Tom gave them a thumbs-up sign.

"We're off."

But they weren't exactly off, Alexandra thought, heart pounding as the plane lurched and lumbered down the rough airstrip. They weren't going to make it off the ground. They were going to just roll their way to Lusaka or wherever they were going.

But just when Alexandra feared they'd never lift, the little red-and-white Piper went airborne—not high but gaining speed and altitude.

Alexandra's hands were damp as she clutched the sides of her cracked leather seat. Her heart was still racing but not as frantically. It'd been scary taking off, and yet now, thousands of feet above the bush, she had such an incredible view of the landscape below that Alexandra laughed, her fear replaced by exhilaration.

This was unreal. By far the most adventurous thing she'd ever done.

"This trip just keeps getting better and better," she said.

Wolf looked at her, dark eyes creased. "I love flying but especially here." He suddenly pointed. "Look. Elephants." And there they were, a huge herd clustered around a grove of waterberry trees.

Alexandra's eyes opened wide. "There must be twenty or thirty of them."

"This is their home."

Their real home, she thought, *their native habitat. Where they belonged.*

As they flew north, Wolf pointed out more game. The giraffes and zebras traveling together. What looked like a lone black rhino. Hundreds of grazing hartebeest and sable.

They'd been traveling for over an hour when Alexandra reached into the backseat to retrieve the water canteen. She was screwing off the top when Wolf silently swore.

She took a quick drink, replaced the cap. "What's wrong?"

"Mmm." He wasn't relaxed anymore and his gaze was fixed on the control panel in front of him.

It was then she realized they were losing altitude. Rapidly.

She glanced at the controls, watched as he clicked the fuel button to the left, the right. She looked up to the fuel gauge. The gauge showed empty. But the tank had been full when they'd left. She saw the gauge, saw him check, knew they'd refueled the plane just this morning.

"Wolf."

"We're going to be landing," he said calmly, as if his announcement was nothing out of the ordinary. "Lock down the canteen and anything loose. Make sure you have nothing sharp in your pockets. Then secure your seat belt. We're about to land."

She shot him another frantic glance as the grassy African plain loomed closer. She couldn't believe this was happening. "You mean *crash.*"

He lightly drew on the yoke, keeping the Piper's nose up. "No," he contradicted her coolly, "I mean land."

CHAPTER TWELVE

CONSIDERING IT WAS A crash landing, Wolf did admirably well trying to keep the wreck of a plane in one piece.

They hit hard, bounced up, came down again. They were rolling, bouncing across the rough terrain, when a huge outcropping of rock threatened to shear them in two.

Wolf slammed on the brakes, pulling hard to the right, and they avoided the rocks but ended up flipping the plane.

Despite bracing herself, Alexandra slammed against the plane's frame as they flipped and then once against the cockpit controls and then finally she dangled in her seat upside down.

"Alexandra," Wolf snapped urgently.

Disoriented, she turned to look at him. Blood trickled down his temple. "I'm okay." She swallowed, dazed.

"You're sure?"

She wiggled her fingers, her ankles, her toes. "Yes." She frowned at him. "But you're bleeding."

"Just a scratch." The urgency had faded from his voice and he worked now to undo his seat belt. It took him just a moment, and then he braced himself, putting a foot and an arm out as he turned himself over and around. Once he was right up, he undid her belt and lifted her out.

Stumbling from the cockpit, Alexandra staggered a few steps on legs that promised to give out. She squinted against the bright sunlight, lifting a weak hand to shield her eyes as she looked to her left and then her right. The savannah stretched in every direction. "Where are we?"

"Based on the plane's compass, I'd say South Luangwa."

"South Luangwa," she repeated numbly, beginning to shiver. It was just shock; she knew it was shock, because she wasn't cold. Not when it had to be at least eighty degrees right now. "Is that a province?"

"It's another national park."

Her head jerked around. "As in, another animal park?"

"Animals don't have parks. They have protected land." Wolf reached into the back of the plane, retrieved the huge duffel bag as well as the knapsack with their lunch and beverages. "We're actually invading their space."

"It's not the invasion I'm worried about. It's personal safety."

"We should be fine. If anything gets too close, we can take shelter in the plane."

She shot the upside down plane a dubious glance. "It's forty years old and covered in fabric. Will it really stop a rhino? Or an elephant?"

"Probably not a charging rhino." He knelt next to the knapsack, found a transmitter radio. "Or an angry elephant bull for that matter." He looked up at her. "But the likelihood of us getting attacked is next to none. This is a six-thousand-acre park. The crash was loud. The animals are running the opposite direction right now."

She compressed her lips. Maybe the impalas and zebras were, but the lions were probably thinking *Yum, yum, fresh meat*. "Does that radio work?"

"I'm going to try to get a signal."

For nearly twenty minutes he worked with the radio, and Alexandra sat next to him, periodically holding her breath, hoping against hope that something miraculous would happen.

Unfortunately they seemed to have run out of miracles for the rest of the day.

Not knowing how long it would be before they were found, Alexandra and Wolf agreed to eat only a fraction of the generous lunch packed. They were already rationing water.

"Where were we going?" Alexandra finally thought to ask as she finished the corner of her meat pie.

"A village north of here." Wolf returned the water canteen to the plane, where it'd stay cooler in the shade. "It's one of the villages I adopted several years ago."

She perched on the red leather bench seat Wolf had taken out of the back of the plane. "How did you adopt a village?"

"Well, some people help sponsor a child in a developing country. I chose to sponsor a village."

She wrapped her arms around her knees, fascinated. "What do you do?"

He shrugged as he dropped onto the ground near her. It was blistering hot out, but they were both trying to take refuge in the shade adjacent to the plane. "Build schools, wells, dig irrigation ditches, develop sanitation facilities, establish medical clinics, provide vaccines, educate about AIDS." He sighed, shook his head. "I'll do whatever I can."

"I had no idea." She felt a wave of tenderness. "That's wonderful. How long have you been doing this?"

"Almost ten years."

"How many villages do you sponsor?"

Uncomfortable, he looked away, dark lashes dropping, concealing his expression. "Not enough," he said at last.

"Tell me—you have to have an idea. Three? Five? Seven?"

"More than twenty. Not quite thirty."

"Thirty villages," she repeated in awe.

His features tightened. He looked pained. "A little money goes a long way out here. There's so much more I want to do, so much more we need to do."

"I think people try, but Africa's a big continent," she said softly. "It's far away, too, and people at home or abroad probably don't know what you know. They haven't seen what you've seen."

"They've an idea," he flashed roughly. "It's all over *Time* and *Newsweek* magazines. The news is always doing segments on children starving and dying—" He broke off, got to his feet. "I'm going to take a short walk. Don't worry, I won't go far."

She watched him set off, his stride long, impatient, angry.

He was gone maybe a half hour, and during the time he was away she sat close to the plane, just in case. But as she sat there, her nervousness gave way to calm.

It was peaceful here, beautiful and golden and serene.

The African savannah was more like Montana than anything she'd ever seen, and it wasn't necessarily the trees and climate as much as the sense of size and openness, the feeling that land and sky stretched endlessly.

She was glad when Wolf returned. His shirt clung wetly to his skin and his hat was damp and dark on his brow. "You look hot," she said.

"I am," he answered, peeling off his shirt and tossing it onto one of the plane's damaged wheels. "Were you scared while I was gone?"

"Not very," she answered, admiring the planes of his chest and his tight, hard abs. He had a gorgeous body, and it was hers. Her husband. She smiled on the inside, happy despite everything. "I like it here."

"In the middle of nowhere?"

"It's not nowhere. It's Africa. Zambia."

The corner of his mouth lifted. "You're a funny girl." He reached into the tail of the plane, muscles rippling and contracting as he rummaged around the back before finding what he was looking for—a battered wood box.

"What's that for?"

"Kindling for tonight's fire," he said, back to rummaging in the tail.

"Wolf, if you quit acting, would you want to direct? Write? Produce?"

"None of the above. I'd be done."

"For a while? A vacation?"

"Forever." He turned from the plane, shot her a dry glance. "I'm sick of L.A., sick of Hollywood, sick of the fake people and fake talk. I want out."

"Where would you go? Dublin?"

"I have a house on the west coast of Ireland. Galway. But I

don't know if I'd move there. Maybe I won't move anywhere. Maybe I'll just bum around, village to village, doing what I can to help."

"You'd sell your house? Your cars—that huge collection?"

"The cars will soon be sold anyway. I buy them, fix them up, sell them at a profit and all proceeds go to one of my charities."

"You've charities, too?"

He nodded yes.

She looked at him for a long time. "Are you really going to leave Los Angeles?"

"Soon. I have to," he said. "It's time. Time to become a real person again. Time to leave the craziness behind."

She leaned forward on the red bench seat, hands balled together. "Wouldn't you miss Hollywood?"

He didn't even hesitate. "No."

Alexandra struggled to think of something to say but nothing came. She couldn't imagine Wolf walking away from Hollywood completely, couldn't imagine him never making another film, never starring in another role. He was too good. Too talented. People enjoyed him so much. "Hollywood would miss you," she said softly.

His laugh was low, cynical. "Only because I make them money."

She shook her head, not thinking about the money or the business but of his talent. He had the rare ability to bring the most complex and disparate characters to life. There were times she used to tell herself Wolf was famous because of his face—his eyes, his mouth, his sex appeal—but not even the most beautiful man could achieve what Wolf had without that rare ability to become another, to become the character, sliding into the skin, feeling the emotions, thinking the thoughts and making even the most vile mortal compelling, fascinating, even sympathetic.

Alex felt a strange tug inside her. Sorrow. Gratitude. Even if he never acted in another film, she'd always be a huge fan. "People will miss you."

He made a rough sound before dragging his hands through

his thick black hair, rifling it on end. "Nothing lasts forever. No one lives forever. All things—even good things—end."

Tears started to her eyes, and Alex turned her head, closed her eyes, willing the tears not to fall. And yet it was a battle, a battle when her chest burned hot, thick with bittersweet emotion. She suddenly pictured the ranch and where she'd been the moment she'd learned her mother had cancer. "So why haven't you walked before?"

Wolf lifted his hands. "I've tried. But the studios…"

He didn't have to finish the explanation. She knew already. The studios wouldn't let him. The studios had too much invested in him.

There would be his agent who wanted his twenty percent. The manager who took another hefty chunk. The publicist and the personal assistants.

The directors who'd already cast him in future films.

The studios themselves who paid bills on the backs of their superstars.

"How long have you felt this way?" she asked, struggling to take it all in, struggling to believe that Wolf really meant what he said.

"Four years. Five."

Five? She swallowed. "And they know this?"

He made a hoarse sound even as the corner of his mouth lifted. "Oh, they know."

"And what do they say?"

His mouth twisted yet again. "What do you think?"

"One more film," she answered softly.

His head inclined. "One more film, just one more, just help us with this, don't let us down, we need you, we need you now, our careers, our lives depend on you."

He snorted, his dark eyes flashing with scorn. "*Their* lives. Talk about greed. People all over the world are dying of hunger, dying for lack of medicine, shelter, lack of the most essential things, and then you have the fat cats in Hollywood talking about *their* lives. It blows me away."

"Not everyone in the industry is loaded. Lots of people—

most of those that actually work on your films—struggle to get by just like everyone else," she said gently.

Some of the tension at his mouth eased. "I know. And that's one of the reasons I continue to work. I know I support a lot of people. But I also know if I stopped acting, they'd find other films, other jobs."

She leaned forward. "If you stopped acting tomorrow, what would you do?"

He didn't even hesitate. "What I'm doing now. I'd help the villages. I'd work with UNICEF, raise more money, raise awareness, become an activist and help anywhere I could."

The sun was just beginning to set when Wolf took a crowbar to the wooden crate, splintering it into medium pieces. Together they gathered some twigs and small branches from a tree near the rocky outcropping.

They put off starting the fire until it was late, eating a half sandwich each and a little of the fruit. And just as Wolf was about to strike the match to light the fire, he looked up and saw Alexandra crouched right next to him, calm, trusting, and he felt as though someone had reached into his chest and ripped his heart out with a violent yank.

What if they couldn't get out of here? What if they ran out of water? Food?

His gaze searched her face, and yet there was no panic in her eyes, no anger or resentment anywhere in her beautiful face. She was more than a good sport. He loved her adventurous attitude almost as much as he loved how genuine she was. How real. She was, he thought, reaching for her, that girl he'd been looking for, the one that reminded him of home.

Wolf cupped her cheek and Alexandra closed her eyes. Just that one touch melted her. Just that one touch made her want incredible things.

She opened her eyes and looked up at him. His eyes were just as endless as the sky above them and even darker.

He wanted her. She felt his desire, felt the need. It was basic and raw. And yet she waited, waiting for him to make the first move.

He touched her mouth with the tip of his finger, gently, lightly stroking down so that her lips burned and tingled, now so sensitive.

Down his fingertip went, over her lower lip to trail down her chin. He traced her jaw and then up to her right earlobe and back across the flushed curve of her cheek.

She was trembling as she stood there, trembling beneath his slow, unhurried touch. She wanted to be caught in his arms, dragged close and kissed until her head spun but he had a different script in mind.

"Kiss me," she breathed, unable to stand it.

"So impatient," he mocked, lowering his head and dropping a brief kiss against her mouth, catching the corner of her lips and the swell of her upper lip.

The brush of his mouth against hers made her belly flip, sending rivulets of fire and ice through her veins.

Shivering, she took a step toward him. "Kiss me again," she urged.

Lifting her up, he carried her to the door of the plane, where he stripped off her clothes and then his and made love to her on what was left of the plane.

Afterward, they stayed inside the plane, and Wolf used some of the blankets from the stash he'd been taking to the village— one for a bed, another for a pillow and the last to cover them.

She lay sleepily against his chest, thinking his body fit hers perfectly. He was hard and strong where she was soft. Stifling a yawn, she thought there'd be no one else, no one that would ever make her feel like this.

Alexandra woke to the feel of Wolf's lips and beard-roughened jaw kissing the back of her neck.

"Good morning," he said.

Sighing contentedly, she scooted closer. "Good morning."

But he wasn't staying in bed. He was getting up. "I'm going to try the radio again. Somebody's got to find us soon."

It was harder to pass the time the second day, at least until Wolf remembered the books, paper, small chalkboards and chalk in the supplies he'd been flying to the village.

With the chalkboards and chalk they began their own version of Twenty Questions. They took turns writing questions down for each other and then they'd turn their chalkboard over and the other would have to answer. Some of the questions were random—what's your favorite color, what's your Chinese zodiac sign, what size shoe do you wear—while others were far more revealing.

"How did you get the name Wolf?" she asked, flashing him her chalkboard. "It's not Spanish or Irish."

"If you were a true fan, you'd know the answer."

She rolled her eyes. "Members of your fan club get the details in a newsletter?"

He laughed appreciatively. "It's a shortened version of my name. I was christened Tynan Wolfe Kerrick. A casting director convinced me to drop Tynan and then the *e* off Wolfe."

"What did your dad call you, then?"

"Tynan."

"And your mom?" she persisted.

The corners of his mouth tilted, and he smiled mockingly up at her from beneath his dense black lashes. "Trouble."

They both laughed and then he held up his board. *Why Hollywood?* it read.

"I've always loved movies," she said. "I was crazy about them as a kid. And not just a little bit but wildly, passionately. It's one of the ways my family helped me cope with losing Mom. They took me to movies every weekend in Bozeman. We didn't have a lot of theatres, so sometimes we'd see the same movie four or five times."

"You have a good family," he said gently.

She nodded thoughtfully. "I do."

"Do you remember your first movie?"

"Disney's *The Little Mermaid*." She smiled shyly. "I remember I cried for Ariel when she lost her voice. And then I cried again at the end, when she and Prince Eric got married—" She broke off, remembering not just that day but all the movies, all the trips to the theater. The way you crunched popcorn and stepped in sticky soda on the way to your seat. The dramatic darkening of the theater as the lights went out. The swish of the curtains opening. The clicking sound the projector made as the movie ended.

She lifted her eyebrows. "I even remember the first movie I saw you in. I was fifteen. You were playing a soldier and you died—" she took a quick breath "—and I cried then, too. And now look at us, stranded here in the middle of nowhere!"

"It's not nowhere," he answered gravely, mimicking her response from yesterday. "It's Zambia. Africa."

She sat nestled in his arms as the sun set, the savannah painted a stunning blood-red, and then the sun disappeared and the horizon turned dark. Not long after, a lion roared in the distance.

Alexandra scrambled to her feet. "I think it's time to light that fire."

"I agree."

Later, as the fire burned, they played their Twenty Questions again, this time without chalkboards since it would be too hard to see. "How old were you when your mom died?" he asked.

Alex leaned forward, pressed her chest against her knees. "Five."

"Are you like her?"

She shook her head. "My brothers say no. They said Mom was sweet—" She broke off, laughed and then took a quick, sharp breath. "I miss her. Being the only girl in my family was hard."

Wolf leaned against one of the red seats from the cockpit and watched her face as she talked. Her face was so expressive in the firelight. Her eyes shone and her mouth curved, twitched, moved, and he thought she just might be the most beautiful woman he'd ever met.

"Mothers are special, aren't they?" he said, grabbing a stalk of dry grass and breaking it off. He rubbed the tall brittle grass between his thumb and finger, twirling it around as though it'd soon take flight.

"I wish I'd been older. Wish I knew her better. Sometimes I'm angry with my brothers because they had so much more time with her. Brock was a senior in high school. Practically an adult." Her eyes filled with tears. She blinked and quickly pushed away the tear. "I was just starting kindergarten. And—" she pushed away another tear "—I don't really remember her. I remember *The Little Mermaid*, but I don't remember her. How's that fair?"

"It's not," he said gently.

"Sometimes I think everything would be so different if my mom were alive today."

He heard the wistfulness in her voice. "How?"

She shrugged. "Maybe I'd be a different person."

"But why would you want to be different? You wouldn't be you—and you're perfect as you are."

Her head ducked and she stared at the fire and then she lifted her head, smiled shyly. "Thank you."

"My pleasure." His gaze held hers, and as the tears dried in her eyes, he knew he hated seeing her cry. He'd do anything to keep her from crying. "So what makes you happy?"

She wrinkled her nose, laughed. "Snow," she whispered. "It reminds me of the movies. It changes everything. Makes simple things beautiful."

And maybe that was her magic, Wolf thought, standing up and holding a hand out to her. She made simple things beautiful, too.

Alexandra was so hungry that night she had a hard time falling asleep. Every time she'd start to doze off, her stomach growled. It was a relief when she did fall into a proper sleep, a deep sleep with a good dream, and she was still in that dream, a place of muted color and muffled sound, when she felt a gust of cold air blow over her.

"Hey, Sleeping Beauty, time to wake up."

Slowly, sleepily she opened her eyes, struggling to focus. "Wolf?"

He was standing outside the plane and he was smiling broadly. "Help has finally arrived."

She sat up so fast she banged her head on the side of the plane. "Seriously?" she demanded, moving to her knees to peek around Wolf. And there was help. A Luangwa park warden in a dusty Land Rover.

She let out a cheer. "We're saved!"

The Luangwa warden had been authorized to drive them to Lusaka, where a massive search-and-rescue party was being organized. They stopped at one of the lodges en route, where they both showered and had a quick meal before continuing on to the capital city.

It took over half the day to get there, and by the time they reached the hotel in downtown, the press had already gathered, their cameras and microphones set up.

As they stepped from the warden's Land Rover there was a cheer, and Daniel was among the first to rush toward them, welcoming them back.

Daniel hugged both. "This is a miracle," he said, wrapping an arm around Alexandra and facing Wolf. "This is better than the best possible scenario." He grinned, but you could see the fatigue etched in deep lines near his eyes. "I don't think I've ever prayed that much in my life."

Wolf clapped a hand on Daniel's back. "We're good, we're fine. Alexandra was a champ."

Daniel shook his head, still overcome. "Joy was hysterical when you didn't return. She feared the worst, but I was sure that you'd make it through somehow. Thank God I was right."

Daniel turned to Wolf, clapped him hard on the back. "My God, am I glad to see you. You can't imagine the chaos or the media frenzy. The studio in Hollywood has been overwhelmed with calls from media all over the world. Reporters and photographers have been rushing to Lusaka from nearly every continent. It's been utter chaos."

Wolf nodded. "Then let's get this press conference over and done with. We're hungry and thirsty and Alexandra's going to want to call her family soon."

Daniel nodded agreement and the three of them approached the makeshift podium where dozens of microphones had been set up. As Daniel made a brief introduction, Alexandra stood behind Wolf, her gaze skimming the crowd of journalists and cameramen.

Then it was Wolf's turn to talk, and he told them about the plane and what he believed caused the crash. He described their two and a half days roughing it in the South Luangwa National Park before being discovered earlier that morning by one of the park wardens.

While Wolf gave them dry details about their stay, information about survival and practical details about food, water and shelter, she recalled something entirely different.

She remembered the deepness of the night, the vastness of the velvet-black sky, the glitter of stars overhead.

She remembered the warmth of Wolf sleeping next to her, his arm curved protectively around her.

She remembered the feel of his hard body on hers, covering her, filling her.

She remembered tenderness. Hunger. Peace.

She remembered love.

Alexandra swallowed around the thickness lodging in her throat.

She'd fallen *in* love with him before they'd ever arrived in Africa, but there, in the South Luangwa National Park, she'd *loved* him. The depth of her feelings for him stunned her, terrified her, left her breathless, speechless. Somehow she'd become his real wife.

Wolf finished speaking, and the crowd of reporters erupted into a frenzy of sound, each journalist shouting to be heard over the other.

"Wolf, did you encounter any animals?"

"What exactly did you eat, Mr. Kerrick?"

"How did you and Mrs. Kerrick manage the extreme heat in the middle of the day?"

"A question for your bride, Wolf. Will you let her speak?"

Wolf turned to Alexandra, extended a hand, encouraging her to join him at the microphones.

Nervously she took his hand and moved to stand beside him. She was trembling—nerves, relief, exhaustion—as she stepped next to Wolf and she feared doing something foolish, embarrassing them both somehow.

But then his arm circled her, his hand resting lightly on her hip, and she was immediately reassured. Calmed. He applied no pressure to her hip, but his touch, his skin was warm and it soothed her. Just being near him she knew that everything would be okay.

But that's how he'd always made her feel.

Even in the beginning. She hadn't wanted to pretend, but Wolf was so magnetic, so compelling, so reassuring that she'd agreed to the part, agreed to the deal.

Crazy. Ridiculous. Miraculous.

She glanced up, looked into his face, seeing the beautifully savage features that made him the world's favorite star. But he wasn't an actor to her. Wasn't a film star or matinee idol. He was just Wolf.

"Are you okay?" he asked, his voice a delicious Irish murmur of sound.

She nodded and, biting her lower lip, realized she meant it. She was okay. Wolf made everything okay.

"How did Wolf handle the crisis, Alexandra?" a reporter shouted.

She looked at Wolf, smiled. "Fine. Better than I did."

"And what did you eat?"

She leaned toward the microphones. "The lodge had sent us with a picnic lunch. It was pretty hearty and we rationed that over the next couple of days."

"Did you plan this, Wolf? Honeymooning on location, plane crash with new bride? Great media news story…"

Wolf laughed wearily. "No. I almost wish I had. It's a good one, isn't it?"

"But that's not exactly true, Wolf." It was Joy who interrupted. Her voice carried, immediately quieting the crowd. Everyone turned to look at her. She'd found a microphone and was standing off to the side. "Meeting and marrying Alexandra Shanahan was a publicity stunt. He did it to end speculation about our relationship."

"Joy." Wolf shook his head, issuing a warning. "No."

She gave him a small, sad smile. "This has to be told, Wolf, it's the only way. The only way you can ever hope to be free." Tears glittered in her eyes. "He never intended to marry Alexandra. He never imagined it'd get that far. But when she got sick, Wolf's such a gentleman he did what he thought was the right thing. He married her. But, Wolf, it's not a real marriage. I know you don't love her. I know you just did this for me."

CHAPTER THIRTEEN

THE PRESS HAD A FIELD day with that one. Talk about tabloid news. Photos were snapped and headlines scribbled and captions created…all while Alexandra stood at the podium, staring aghast at Wolf.

Was Joy right? Was what she'd just said true?

Even as reporters erupted in shouts, Wolf grabbed Alexandra's hand and hustled her away from the pandemonium and into the hotel, where a suite had been reserved for them.

It was the royal suite, the hotel day manager said, handing them the keys, in honor of their esteemed guests. But Wolf barely answered and Alexandra was downright catatonic.

On the top floor, in their room, Wolf made Alexandra sit. "Listen to me," he said roughly. "I will tell you this one time and I need you to listen and believe me." His accent deepened, growing more pronounced with his exhaustion and stress.

"There is nothing between Joy and me. We're friends," he continued. "Only friends. People have always made it out to be more, but that's because people have an insatiable need for scandal."

"But Joy said—"

"I don't care what Joy said. I'm telling you the truth. And it's me you need to believe. I'm your husband. I'm the one you turn to when you need something, when you doubt, when you question sanity. It's me. Understand?"

Her lower lip trembled and she bit into it ruthlessly, biting down so hard she tasted blood.

"Joy's not a happy person," Wolf continued. "She's struggled for years with booze and pills and bouts of depression. Try to realize she's suffering right now and anything she says or does is because she's in pain."

Alexandra covered her face to keep him from seeing how his words hurt. She knew he thought he was helping. She knew he thought he was making everything clear. But he didn't realize a woman wanted more than a sexually faithful husband. A woman needed her man to be emotionally faithful, too.

Wolf crouched in front of her and pulled her hands away from her face. "Why are you crying?"

"Because I'm afraid."

His dark eyes were tormented. "Of what? Me?"

And then the tears fell. Because she wasn't afraid of him, not physically, but she was afraid he'd never give her what she needed most. "I can't compete for you."

"You don't have to."

"But I feel like I do. I feel like I could lose you any moment."

He let her go then and slowly stood. "If you feel that way, you'll make it happen. You will lose me because you'll think it into reality."

She reached out for him, hands up, pleading. "Am I not here? Am I not saying Wolf, help me make this work?"

"Listen to me, Alexandra. I am here and I want to make this work, too." He returned to her, pulled her up into his arms and stroked her wet cheeks with his thumbs. "You're not alone in this." His voice fell, deepened. He touched his mouth to hers. "I want to be with you."

And when they made love, it was so good and so tender and so raw and real it hurt.

Wolf was right for her in so many ways. Wolf was everything she'd ever wanted in a man. But still a small part of her was afraid. She could fight Joy when it was the two of them, Alexandra and Wolf. But when Wolf went through the door, he was out there on his own.

And maybe that's what she feared. His judgment. His inability to take a stand, a side.

Her side.

Lying next to Wolf, she watched him sleep, his impossibly thick lashes like ebony crescents on his cheeks.

Tomorrow he'd go back to work, and then what?

But they woke the next day to even more bad news.

The producers pulled the plug on the film. They were ordering all crew and cast back home.

There'd been problems with the project from the beginning, but Joy's highly televised outburst was the final straw. Alexandra tried to talk about it with Wolf, but he just shook his head, unable to communicate.

They spent the afternoon killing time, sightseeing in Lusaka. And then the next morning Alexandra and Wolf boarded the British Airways jet and headed home.

Back in California they returned to Wolf's Malibu house. After Africa, the house felt strange, too big, too new, too modern. But they hadn't been home even a day before Joy started calling.

Alexandra told herself they were just phone calls. She told herself to let it go, not to care. She remembered Wolf's explanations, remembered how he'd seemed sincere, and it worked. At first.

But the phone calls didn't stop. She'd phone him on his mobile or at the house and she'd be crying. She'd be inconsolable. Wolf would take the phone into his office at the back of the house and have endless conversations with her.

Wolf told Alexandra that Joy was upset about the film being shelved. She was worried she'd alienated them. She worried that the public blamed her for any problems in Wolf and Alexandra's marriage.

It was always on the tip of Alexandra's tongue to say, "Yes, she does cause problems." But she knew it'd only antagonize Wolf, so she bit her tongue and didn't complain.

But the weeks passed and the calls continued and Wolf grew more distracted. They still made love, but in some ways Wolf wasn't quite there anymore. It wasn't that the pleasure was gone, but the emotional intensity had changed. Faded.

And it tormented her, it really did.

After making love one night, Wolf fell into an immediate deep sleep, and after lying there sleepless, Alexandra finally got up. She went to the kitchen to get something to eat, and Wolf's mobile phone was there on the counter. She hated this phone, she thought. It might as well be Joy's phone.

Glancing down, she saw he had a missed call.

Joy, probably.

And suddenly desperate to know just how bad this was, Alexandra clicked on his phone's call list and scanned through the incoming calls from just today. New York, New York, New York, all the same number. Joy's number.

She scrolled down through the entire in-box. Joy. Joy. Joy. Joy.

She clicked on his out-box, checked numbers dialed.

Joy. Joy. Joy. Joy.

Covering her mouth, she sat down on a stool at the counter and tried to keep her scream from coming out.

She was losing him. She was losing him and she couldn't seem to stop it, change it, do anything about it.

"Alexandra." It was Wolf standing in the kitchen doorway.

She couldn't even turn to look at him or he'd see the suffering in her face. "I think we're in trouble here, Wolf. Things aren't going so well."

"Want to talk about it?"

She shook her head and pushed his phone back and forth on the counter. "Talking's not helping. In fact, when you and I talk, things just seem to get worse."

He cleared his throat. "In bed, earlier, everything was fine."

She almost laughed. In bed. Of course a man would think that way. And then she closed her eyes to keep the hurt in. "I'm running out of steam, Wolf. I'm thinking this isn't going the way it needs to go." She swallowed around the lump filling her throat. "Not for me. Nor you."

"It has been hard, Alex. But it'll get easier soon."

"Why? Is Joy seeing a doctor? Taking a new antidepressant? What makes you think any of this will ever change?"

"She's working to fix her problems, yes."

Alexandra slammed her hands onto the counter. "But aren't we all? My God, Wolf, what about me? Can't you see I'm having problems? Can't you see I'm hurt? Can't you see I need you, too? Maybe even need you more?"

"Alex."

"No." She dashed away the tears. "Please, please don't do that anymore. Don't sigh like I'm the difficult one. Don't make me feel like I'm being unreasonable to want to have my husband's attention."

"How many times do I have to tell you, you have me?"

"All right, then answer me this." She balled her fist against the cool counter. "If Joy called you tomorrow and said she needed you, you'd go." She lifted her head, looked at him. "Wouldn't you?"

"I'd help any friend that needed me."

"Then help me," she whispered, her gaze holding his. "Pick me."

He'd frozen in place. She hadn't said the actual words yet, hadn't even planned on saying the words, but suddenly it was there, the nuance.

She was about to draw the battle lines. Demand his loyalty. Define the boundaries.

"What are you saying?" he asked, expression shuttered.

What was she saying? she wondered. Did she really know what she was saying? Her thoughts spun. She struggled to gain control before the situation got out of hand. She was tired, worn down, emotional. Did she really want to do this now?

"Alexandra?" he prompted.

"Maybe it's time we settled things once and for all," she said, so cold on the inside that she felt like a puppet, oddly detached. "Maybe we should just say what needs to be said."

His expression grew increasingly wary. "And what needs to be said?"

Her eyes burned. She swallowed. "Who do you want? Joy or me?"

"Alexandra..."

"Wolf, I need to know. If you were to pick only one of us, would it be her or me?"

"It doesn't work like that," he said impatiently. "You're my wife. And Joy, she's…she's a friend and troubled, and the situation's complicated."

Complicated?

Why was his love so complicated? How could it be so complicated? Love wasn't complicated for her. She knew who she loved and she knew why she loved and she knew that as long as Wolf was in her life he was her priority. It was as complicated—or simple—as that.

"I've put you first," she said flatly. "From the beginning I've put you first. Now do the same for me—"

"Alexandra."

"Wolf, I can't handle this anymore."

He looked at her so long she felt her heart slow and her insides gel. He looked at her with pain and exhaustion, sorrow and frustration. And she realized he wasn't going to give her what she wanted. Wasn't going to give her what she needed.

"I'll pack my things," he said quietly. "I have a trip to Venice in a few days. I'll just leave early."

"So that's your decision?" she choked out, chilled.

"I'm sick of the pressure, Alexandra. I can't be who or what you want me to be and I'm worn out from trying, too."

Wolf drew a suitcase out from the walk-in closet and began to pack. She watched him in stunned silence. He was packing so fast he was almost throwing clothes into the bag.

"You're really going to go?" she whispered, sinking down onto the foot of the bed. She could barely breathe as she watched him pack. Her pulse raced and her heart squeezed up into her throat.

He shoved his leather wash kit into the bag. "I didn't get to where I am by playing nice and lining up straight and following rules. But at the same time, I'm loyal and honorable and I protect those I love."

"Do you love Joy?"

Wolf paused, head lifting, dark eyes finding hers. "What is it with you and Joy? She's a bloody alcoholic. Alcoholism is a disease and you're damn lucky not to have it."

His words only made her ache more. She swallowed the lump in her throat, swallowed back the hurt. He was packing shoes now, a belt, and he'd pulled his tuxedo out and was slipping that into a hanging garment bag.

"Wolf."

"What?" he snapped, zipping the garment bag closed.

She blinked back the tears threatening to fall. She wished he'd turn around, wished he'd at least look at her. He didn't.

She slid off the bed and gently, lightly, put her hand on his back, feeling the taut muscles, the tension in his spine. "I'm sorry."

"I'm not so sure you are," he said coldly as he grabbed his bag and walked away.

She watched him in disbelief. He was leaving. Like that. No kiss, no touch, nothing warm or reassuring.

What the hell had happened? Since Zambia Wolf had been different. Changed.

Alexandra hurried after Wolf, trailing him down the staircase to the hall below. "Is it over then?" Alexandra cried as he reached to open the garage door. "Are we finished?"

Wolf stopped. His broad shoulders nearly filled the door frame, casting a long, dark shadow behind him. "I don't know."

She pressed a hand to her chest, her heart beating so hard it hurt. "Do you want a divorce?"

He said nothing, choosing to remain silent, and his silence was worse than any words. Rage and pain and heartbreak filled her.

"*Wolf?*" she demanded, even though she already knew the answer. But she wanted to hear it from him, wanted him to finally speak the truth.

Slowly his head turned. She could just glimpse the hard line of his cheekbone, the curve of his ear. "I don't know. I need time. I need to think."

The words broke what was left of her heart. Hot, furious emotion rushed through her. The emotions were wild, the pain extreme. He'd made her feel safe. He'd made her feel loved. He'd made her believe he'd be there for her and with her and that it was okay to love him. It was okay to fall in love with him. It was okay to imagine a life together. But it was all a lie. He'd lied. He'd pretended. He'd *acted*.

"You tricked me," she choked out, taking a step toward him. "You deceived me."

He said nothing.

Her hands balled convulsively. Tears blinded her. Hysteria, rage, grief bubbled, boiled. "If you go and leave me, Wolf, I won't be here when you return."

And still he said nothing.

The pain and his silence whipped at her, tormenting her. *"Wolf."*

"I hear you, Alexandra. You don't have to shout."

She was wiping the tears away, one after the other. "If you go to Venice now, I won't be here when you come back," she repeated in a whisper. "I won't."

He nodded. And then he left.

Alexandra crawled into bed after he left, carrying the house phone and the mobile phone with her, just in case Wolf changed his mind. Just in case he called.

She didn't leave the house in case he changed his mind.

But night came, and the Europe flights were all gone. And when she turned on the television the next morning there was a story about the Venice Film Festival and the glittering guest list, with Wolf Kerrick and Joy Hughes making their first appearance together since the dramatic plane crash and rescue in Zambia.

And then suddenly there they were, Wolf and Joy, arriving at the Venice airport, filmed amid a blinding strobe of flashes. Joy wore an enormous mink coat over her jeans and turtleneck sweater, while Wolf was in his favorite jeans and a T-shirt topped with a wool coat. They looked gorgeous together, Alexandra thought, the way a celebrity couple should look.

Turning off the television, Alexandra knew it was time to pack, find a place of her own, return to work and move on.

* * *

In the first month after separating from Wolf, Alexandra was so overwhelmed trying to adjust to a different life, settling into her new home—a condo close to downtown Los Angeles in a new development filled with artists, writers and trendy business executives—and learning the ropes of her new job that she didn't really let herself think about the end of their relationship.

But later, as the newness wore off and the pattern of her days emerged, her work became more routine and she grew comfortable reading scripts, meeting with studio heads and acting as the intermediary between directors, actors and producers. People took her seriously. Her opinions were respected. And before long her name was added to the credits of her first film as an assistant director. It was a huge personal moment for Alexandra. She wasn't just a coffee girl anymore but a valuable member of a studio making major motion pictures.

That night she took Kristie and some of the other girls from the studio's front office out to dinner at the Ivy and they celebrated. Alexandra promised Kristie and the others that if they wanted to get out of copy-room hell, she'd do everything she could to help them, and she meant it.

It was a lovely dinner, warm, happy, full of laughter and enthusiasm. After four and a half years in Los Angeles, Alexandra finally felt as though she belonged. She'd made it. She could live here, survive here and be happy here.

Even without Wolf.

But back home later that night, after Alexandra entered her dimly lit condo, she walked to the enormous plate-glass window in the living room with its view of downtown. The skyscrapers were lit and the streets below were dotted with yellow lights. She felt a pang of such sorrow and loss it nearly doubled her.

She realized she'd never really accepted that the relationship was over. In the back of her mind she'd secretly thought that maybe, just maybe, it could be saved. But it hadn't worked out that way.

After Wolf's Venice trip, he went to London for six weeks, where he filled in for an actor in a West End play. When the play closed, he engaged in a series of meetings with the producers of *The Burning Shore* and eventually, by promising to put up his own money and coming onto the picture as a coproducer, he got the studio to agree to finish the film. Wolf had gone back to Africa.

Alexandra sank down on the arm of her sofa, her stomach falling along with her heart.

Until now she'd hoped, secretly hoped, it would just be a matter of time before Wolf returned to her. She'd thought that after he finished in Zambia he'd call or come see her. She'd imagined that being in Zambia would remind him of her, of the experiences they'd shared, and he'd realize he missed her. Loved her. And wanted her.

But it'd been months since the filming had wrapped, and instead of returning to California, Wolf had sold his Malibu home and bought a house in the outskirts of Dublin.

Sitting on the arm of her sofa, Alexandra was forced to confront the reality that Wolf was never coming back. At least not for her. And despite her best efforts to put on a brave face, focus on her career and begin to move forward, she'd only managed to do the above because she'd thought soon she and Wolf would be together again and everything would eventually be fine.

But Wolf wasn't coming back and they weren't going to be together again and somehow, she thought, reaching up to catch a tear before it fell, she had to believe that everything would still be fine.

But to make everything truly finished, she had to take the next step, the step she dreaded, the one that would legally separate them. Neither had taken any action to dissolve their marriage, and Alexandra had thought it was because Wolf still loved her. But maybe it wasn't love that kept them legally bound but public relations.

Maybe he was waiting for her to be the one to file, to initiate the divorce proceedings, to preserve his image. His precious reputation.

If she filed, she'd be the bad girl and he'd remain the hero.

Eyes hot and gritty, Alexandra moved to the computer at the desk in her kitchen nook. She pulled the keyboard out on the granite counter and clicked on her e-mail account and then Wolf's e-mail address.

Wolf, she typed quickly, I wanted you to be the first to know that I'm filing for divorce tomorrow. I'm not asking for spousal support or a settlement. I wish you well always. Alexandra

She read and reread her brief message, hoping it sounded relatively cordial. She wanted to be fair and calm and nonemotional. Twice she went to add another line, something more personal and then less personal, but eventually she just gave up and pressed send, whisking the message from her out-box to his in-box.

The next day she used her lunch break to drive to the county courthouse, where she filled out the necessary paperwork. After signing her name, she submitted the forms to the clerk. The clerk stamped her paperwork and gave her a receipt.

"If it's uncontested," the clerk said, "in six months you'll receive a letter confirming the dissolution."

Alexandra nodded, thanked the clerk and turned away.

And that, she said silently, a massive lump swelling in her throat, is *the end of that.*

Two weeks later, Alexandra had been invited to attend an industry party, one of those gala events she'd been so in awe of a year ago. After her brief marriage to Wolf and her new position at Paradise Pictures, industry parties felt normal.

As she stepped from the limo—the studio always sent a limo for her when she attended events and she'd wondered more than once if that was Wolf's doing—camera flashes briefly blinded her. She stood next to the car for a moment in her snug deep blue satin evening gown and smiled, the deep plunging V neckline showing off the creamy skin between her breasts, the neckline accented with a romantic satin ruffle that caught the light and shimmered like midnight with a full moon.

She'd started to move on when photographers shouted out, pleading with her for just another picture, so Alexandra paused again, shoulders squared, stomach pulled in flat, and forced another smile, the firm, confident smile she'd seen countless celebrities do. As she held her position, she realized Wolf had been right. She'd become a celebrity by virtue of association. Once she'd married him, she'd earned an elite Hollywood status. And although they now lived on separate continents, she was still Mrs. Wolf Kerrick around town.

And there were nights like tonight when, despite the physical distance between them, Alexandra almost believed that Wolf was near. It was as though he were still part of her life, aware of her world and the things she was doing.

Or maybe that was just wishful thinking, she thought, clutching her black handbag—the same one she'd carried that very first night she and Wolf had gone out together for drinks at the Casa Del Mar—and headed in.

Inside the hotel's ballroom doors, she was handed a flute of champagne. As she moved through the crowd, she heard bits and pieces of peoples' conversations. It was mid-June and the big summer blockbusters were just starting to be released. Everyone had something to say about the summer films as well as the need to get box-office revenue up again. For the fourth year in a row attendance was down and industry insiders were worried. People just weren't going to movies the way they used to despite the increasing number of choices. What would it take to get people back to theaters again?

Across the ballroom she spotted Daniel deVoors at the same time he saw her. He lifted his flute in acknowledgment. She smiled and planned to cross the enormous room in a little bit to visit with him.

Like Wolf, Daniel had returned to Africa to finish filming *The Burning Shore*. The film was in postproduction now, slated as a Christmas release. The heavyweight films, the ones considered to be Oscar contenders, were usually released in December and January in order to be fresh in Academy members' minds at nomination time. Wolf, it was rumored, would be up for another Academy Award as best actor. Daniel would be up for best director, and it was said that Joy would probably earn her first nomination for best actress.

Moving through the crowded ballroom toward Daniel,

Alexandra knew that even though she found it painful to think about Wolf, she was happy for him—as well as the cast and crew—that the picture had finally come together. It wasn't even his financial investment she cared about. Rather, she knew how much he loved Africa and the story and the people there. She was proud that he'd made something so problematic work. He'd really fought for the film, and it'd paid off.

Daniel shifted in the crowd, and as he moved to one side, she felt an icy shaft of pain and heartbreak.

Wolf. He was here.

Pulse leaping, she drank him in—tall, darkly handsome, dressed in a black tuxedo with a black dress shirt and no bow tie, of course. His hair was longer—considerably longer, nearly down to his shoulders—and the style made him look even more fierce and primitive and male. Then he reached out and drew the woman next to him closer to his side.

Joy.

Her heart squeezed into a tattered ball and then fell, a dramatic free fall all the way to the tips of her navy satin pumps.

He was here. With Joy.

She couldn't move, couldn't take another step, and for the first time since arriving at the hotel she felt grateful for the crowd surging around her. She needed them, all these people, to buffer her, keep her from falling, fainting, weeping.

Instead she stood there, rooted to her spot, and felt pain roll. Pain and loss and rejection. The emotions were so intense she knew they had to show on her face. She wasn't an actress, couldn't hide her feelings, not feelings this strong, and she prayed no one saw how once again her heart was breaking.

Seeing Wolf and Joy together tonight was nothing short of excruciating. She'd never heard back from Wolf after she'd filed the divorce papers, but the media had somehow managed to get a copy of the paperwork and *People* magazine had run a color copy of the front page of the form. There in an enormous picture was her request to end her marriage. The headline to the accompanying article was every bit as salacious as she'd feared. And still no word from Wolf.

But now here he was, a dozen yards away, with Joy. And even if she believed that Joy and Wolf had never been lovers, the fact that Wolf still saw Joy and spent time with her cut, and cut deeply.

Alexandra envied Joy and Wolf's bond. It was obvious they had a special connection, and standing there, watching them, Alexandra had never felt like such an outsider as she did just then.

Someone bumped her from behind and she finally forced herself to move, slipping as quickly through the crowd as she could.

With a frozen smile fixed to her face she prayed no one could see how much she was hurting. Cameras were everywhere. The last thing she wanted was photos in tomorrow's paper showing her leaving the fund-raiser in tears.

And yet, as she slid into the backseat of the limo, her frozen smile shattered and tears filled her eyes.

She'd loved him. Trusted him. And it'd broken her heart.

CHAPTER FOURTEEN

IT WAS A LONG, ENDLESS, sleepless night. She cried off and on, getting up once to wash her face, and by the time her alarm finally went off, Alexandra felt as though she'd gone thirteen rounds in a heavyweight fight.

After dressing and downing a cup of strong black coffee, she dragged herself to work feeling half-alive.

Even though she felt like hell, the front office was buzzing with excitement. Apparently Wolf had been in there early for a brief meeting with one of the studio's heads. Kristie had seen Wolf on her way in—he'd just been leaving—and she was telling the other girls that he'd looked even more gorgeous than usual.

"His hair's long now," she whispered dramatically. "And it makes him look wicked and unbelievably sexy."

Alexandra carried her mug of herbal tea past the giggling office staff to her desk in the back. Her promotion had meant a private office, and it wasn't big but it was at least quiet with the door shut.

Taking a seat at her desk, she turned on her computer, checked e-mail, answered the ones requiring an immediate response and then got busy reading the script needing her attention first.

She didn't know how long she'd been reading when she felt the oddest shivery sensation, like that of a feather being trailed across her skin. Reaching up, she rubbed at her nape, where the skin felt most sensitive. All the hairs on her arms were standing up, as well.

It was then she realized she wasn't alone. Wolf was standing just inside her door.

For a long moment she simply stared at him. He looked like a pirate with his long black hair and his dark, shadowed jaw.

"Your hair's so long," she said almost absently.

"It's for my next role. Blackbeard."

"He was vile."

Creases fanned at his eyes. "Brilliant."

"Cruel."

"Practical."

"Insensitive."

"Legendary."

Alexandra fell silent. She wasn't going to win. Wolf was Wolf. He'd always be smarter, faster, stronger, richer, more beautiful.

His jaw jutted at an angle and his dark lashes dropped, concealing his eyes. "You left quickly last night, before we could speak."

Her heart ached fiercely. "There was no reason for us to speak."

He didn't move, and yet she felt his physical presence grow, his anger and leashed tension filling the room. "There's our marriage."

"Divorce," she corrected.

"I've contested the divorce."

Alexandra grabbed at the edge of her desk, reeling. "You what?"

"I'm Irish and Spanish. I don't believe in divorce."

"But this is California."

"And you married me. And maybe I'm vile and cruel and insensitive, but I view marriage as a holy union—"

"Really? Then where the hell have you been?" She slapped her hands on her desktop, hitting the surface so hard her tea sloshed a little in the white ceramic mug. "I certainly wouldn't say you've been doing anything to try to save the marriage."

"You gave me an ultimatum," he said unapologetically.

"So you leave and never contact me again?"

He shrugged. "I was giving you time."

"To hate you!"

His dark eyes flashed. Lines etched at his mouth. "Hate's a sister emotion to love."

She shook her head. She couldn't do this, not now, not here, not like this. She hadn't gotten any sleep last night. Her head ached from crying.

For the past months she'd done everything she could to stabilize herself, to make her new world okay. And to do that, she'd had to minimize Wolf, reduce his influence and the impact he had on her.

When his name was mentioned on television or she came across one of his movies on cable, she turned the channel. When the papers printed an interview, she skipped it. When people at parties mentioned him, she moved to another group gathered. It wasn't that she was bitter, it was just that everything to do with him—them—still hurt. Even after the end of their relationship, even after filing for divorce, her heart still felt broken.

Leaving the party last night she'd felt destroyed. She'd felt empty. Different. Changed. And she didn't like these feelings at all, didn't like the helplessness they entailed. "This isn't the time, Wolf," she said woodenly. "I'm working—"

"And work is more important than us? Than our marriage, our family?"

She drew a rough breath. "We were never a family."

"We could have been. We could have had a good life, a great life—"

"How? With you on the road? Movie after movie, always setting out, going on location, playing the lead against another Hollywood ingenue?"

His mouth tightened and deep grooves shaped his lips while finer lines creased his eyes. "So this isn't really about Joy, is it? It was never as much Joy as your own insecurity."

Alexandra just looked at him, eyes dry, head throbbing, heart in pieces.

"I've spent the past months analyzing what the hell happened," he added. "And I never really understood where it fell apart or why it had to. I loved you. I would have done anything for you—"

"You chose Joy over me!"

"I chose to stand by Joy while she struggled with a brutal disease that could have destroyed her career the same way it destroyed her marriage."

"But you should have stood by me."

His expression turned furious. "I did. I'm here. I contested the divorce." He slugged his fist against the door frame. "Why are you so bloody insecure? Because that's the real issue, isn't it? It's not me making films or traveling and going on location, but you're afraid of other women. You're so afraid I'll fall for another woman that you're shutting me out, not even giving us a chance to succeed."

Her eyes opened wide. Her stomach rose, up into her throat.

My God, he knew her. He knew her too well.

He knew exactly what she was afraid of, and that knowledge knocked her off balance.

With trembling fingers Alexandra pushed her mug across her desk. She couldn't look at him, couldn't face him now. "It would kill me if I found out through the newspapers or tabloids that you'd found someone else. And, Wolf, it'd happen. Sooner or later. It's bound to happen—"

"Why?"

"Because I'm ordinary. I'm not like you."

She felt rather than heard him leave. And his abrupt departure created an even more violent loss than what she'd felt before.

Alexandra was still sitting numbly at her desk when her phone rang. Dazed, she picked it up.

Her brother Troy was at the other end of the line. "Alexandra, Dad's had a heart attack. Please come home."

Troy sent his jet for her and she boarded the plane in Burbank, at the executive terminal there. It was a two-and-a-half-hour flight to Bozeman, Montana, and her oldest brother, Brock, was waiting for her at the Bozeman airport to drive her to the hospital where her father was in ICU.

Brock wrapped her in a huge bear hug and kissed her cheek. "We've missed you, little girl," he said, stepping back to look her over.

She nodded around the lump in her throat. "I've missed you, too." Alexandra pushed a long wave of hair back from her face. "How's Dad?"

Brock shrugged as he lifted her bag. "As good as can be hoped."

She knew from Brock's tone that Dad wasn't doing well. They were walking to Brock's truck now and she had to practically run to keep up with his long strides. "And the kids?" she asked, referring to his children, fraternal twins Molly and Mack.

"They'll be thrilled to see you." He shot her a hard look. "You know, it was hard for them losing you and their mom so close together."

"Brock, they were babies when I left. And you weren't even living at the ranch anymore. You and Amy had your own place then."

He shrugged again. "I'm just saying."

She knew what he was saying. He wasn't any different from Troy or Trey or Dillon or Cormac. She was the girl in the family. It had been her responsibility to keep things together. And Alexandra hadn't wanted that responsibility. She was the youngest. She hardly even knew who she was, and being the only woman nearly smothered her at times.

At the hospital, Alexandra leaned over her father's bed. He had an oxygen tent around him and tubes and wires running every which way. "Daddy," she whispered, covering his hand with hers. "Daddy, I'm here."

For a moment she thought he hadn't heard her, but then his eyes briefly opened and he looked at her for a second. "Good," he sighed heavily. "I'm glad you're home."

Alexandra sat by his side until twilight, when Dillon, the youngest of her brothers, appeared and told her Brock was waiting downstairs to take her back to the ranch. "I'll stay with Dad until midnight. That's when Cormac will come," he added, giving her a quick hug and a peck on the forehead. "Now go see your niece and nephew. They're desperate to see Aunt Alex."

Brock wasn't the only one in the truck. Molly and Mack were there, too, and they wiggled like puppies as she climbed in the passenger seat.

"How's Grandpa?" Molly asked, big-eyed in the backseat. "Is he talking yet?"

Alexandra managed a small smile. "Not a lot yet, but he knows we're there."

It was a forty-minute drive back to the ranch and dark by the time they reached the two-story stone-and-wood house. Cormac was waiting on the front steps when the truck appeared in the long, dusty drive.

As Alexandra stepped from the truck, he scooped her in another Shanahan death-grip hug. The Shanahans were Black Irish, all tall, dark and rugged, but Cormac was the exception. He was the only blonde one in the batch, and it was Cormac her friends all used to have crushes on.

The housekeeper had dinner waiting. And after dinner, with six-year-old Molly sitting on her lap, Alexandra played Mack— Cormac's namesake—in a game of checkers. Mack at six could already trounce her, and like a true Shanahan, he crowed with pleasure. Molly looked at Alexandra and made a face. "Boys," she said with six-year-old disgust.

Alexandra winked. "I agree."

After she read to the kids and put them to bed, she returned downstairs and walked in on a conversation she obviously wasn't supposed to hear as Cormac and Brock both went quiet.

"What?" she said, looking from one to the other. "What's wrong? Is it Dad? Has he gotten worse?"

Cormac shook his head. "No. Dad's stable. It's Wolf." He hesitated. "He's on the way."

Alexandra's forehead furrowed. *Wolf? On his way here? To the ranch?* "That's a mistake. How did you hear this? Who told you? Was this in a paper or something?"

"I just talked to him on the phone," Brock said. "He called to check on Dad."

Alexandra couldn't believe it. She looked from Brock to Cormac. "But that doesn't mean he's coming here."

Brock shrugged. "He said he was."

"When?"

"I don't know." He looked at her more closely. "Why? Is there a problem? Wolf said everything was all patched up."

"All patched up?" Alexandra felt like weeping with frustration. "That's what he said?"

"That's what he said."

In her old bedroom, Alexandra tried dialing Wolf's cell number, but he didn't pick up. Each time she called she got his voice mail. "Wolf," she said on the fifth call, "it's Alexandra. Brock said you're coming here. I don't think that's a good idea. Please call me back."

But he didn't call back, and Alexandra knew that was not good.

She was still sitting on her bed in the dark, clutching her phone, when Brock knocked on the door on his way to bed.

"Did you reach him?" Brock asked gruffly, standing in her bedroom door.

"No." She cleared her throat. She didn't want him to know she'd been crying. "I just kept getting his voice mail."

"He might already be on his way."

That's exactly what she was afraid of.

"You're lucky," her brother said bluntly. "He still cares about you. He wouldn't be coming here if he didn't."

"It's not that easy," she answered, feeling defensive.

"That's pride talking, little girl. It's time you did some forgiving and forgetting. He's just a man, and all men make mistakes."

Chilled on the inside, she wrapped her arms around her knees, trying to get warm. "But he's not just any man. He's a star, a huge star, and gorgeous. And I'm nothing like him and I can't keep up with him or compete with the women who throw themselves at him—"

"So you're just going to quit your marriage? Just like that?" A contemptuous note had entered his voice.

"It hurts!" She blinked back fresh tears. "And being afraid and worried hurts, too. I hate that feeling. I hate not knowing—"

"But you do know. You know he loves you and you know he wants to be married to you. And, little girl, I hate to disappoint you, but there are no real guarantees in life. There's just our hearts and our hopes and learning to live one day at a time." His voice dropped, roughened. "If I'd known Amy was going to die two years after our wedding, do you think I would have married her? If I'd known we'd have two babies who would grow up without a mother, do you think I would have conceived them?"

Even in the dark she heard and felt Brock's grief. It was still there, five and a half years after Amy's death. He'd loved her since he'd first laid eyes on her.

"Yes," she whispered, wiping away a tear in the dark. "She was made for you."

Brock didn't speak, and she saw his head bow, his silhouette filling the doorway.

"Yes," he agreed, "she was made for me. Just like your Wolf was made for you." Brock reached for the doorknob, started to pull the door closed but stopped partway.

"There's worse things than being afraid, Alex. There's losing your heart altogether." And then he stepped into the hall and quietly, gently, closed her bedroom door behind him.

Wolf had a hell of a time finding the Lazy L ranch. Everyone knew the Shanahans, but that didn't make locating the property entrance easy. He'd called Brock last night to check on Alexandra's father and get directions, and while Brock hadn't told him not to come, he certainly hadn't been encouraging.

But Brock's lack of enthusiasm didn't stop Wolf from flying up first thing the next morning.

Now he was parking in front of the huge split-logs-and-stone house, and as he climbed from the four-by-four Jeep, the front door of the house opened and out trooped three of Alexandra's brothers. Brock, Cormac and Dillon.

They weren't, Wolf noted, catching sight of their grim faces, very welcoming either.

"I'm here for Alexandra," he said, letting the Jeep door slam behind him.

"She's with Dad," Brock answered. "In Bozeman, at the hospital."

Wolf shrugged. "I'll wait for her here then."

"She doesn't want to see you," Dillon said flatly.

Wolf shrugged. "I'm still waiting."

Cormac folded his arms across his chest. "Maybe you should wait in Los Angeles. She knows where to find you there, doesn't she?"

"No, actually. I don't live in Los Angeles anymore. So if it's all right with you—" and his smile was predatory, antagonistic "—I'll just wait here until she returns."

Cormac's eyes narrowed. "Maybe you didn't hear me. She's not here. And even if she were, she doesn't want to see you. I suggest you get back in your car and go home."

Wolf drew a deep breath. It'd been a long morning. It was going to be a long afternoon and night. "I'll wait for Alexandra."

The front door of the house opened again and this time Troy and Trey appeared. The twins had come home to the Lazy L ranch, too. Their dad must be very sick for all five brothers to have returned now, especially when three of them lived out of state in metropolitan places like New York, San Francisco and Seattle.

"You're still here?" Troy drawled, moving to stand next to his brothers. "I thought you were told to leave."

Any other time Wolf would have admired their family loyalty. Right now he just wanted to see Alexandra. "Your dad's sick. This isn't the time for this—"

"You should have thought of that before you broke Alexandra's heart," Trey said coldly.

Wolf shook his head. He wasn't going to get anywhere with the Shanahan brothers using words. "I want to talk to Alexandra and you don't want me to. What do I have to do to get a few minutes alone with her?"

"Nothing," Dillon said. "It's not happening. Not unless you go through me."

"And me," Brock added.

Trey stepped forward. "Count me in. That's three."

"Four," Troy chimed.

Wolf looked drily at Cormac. "What about you? Thinking about joining my side, evening up the odds a little?"

Cormac checked his smile, shook his head. "Sorry, Kerrick, I'm with them. That makes five."

Wolf studied the lineup of Shanahan brothers. "You don't really mean to keep your sister from me."

Troy jammed his hands into his jean pockets. "We do."

Wolf nodded once, slow and thoughtful. "Let me get this right. If I fight all of you, you'll give me a few minutes alone with my wife?"

"You fight all five of us and you'll get five minutes."

Wolf glanced from one brother to another. "So where are we going to do this? Outside or in the barn?"

Brock sighed. "The barn will work just fine."

As soon as Alexandra spotted the silver rental Jeep parked in front of the house, her stomach tightened up, a flurry of nerves, hope and fear. Wolf. He'd arrived. For a brief moment she considered turning around and heading straight back to Bozeman. Instead she parked. And as she turned off the ignition she thought of her dad—widowed young with six kids, one just entering kindergarten—and her brother Brock who at thirty became a single father to twin infants overnight.

She'd experienced enough loss in her own family to know there weren't any guarantees, and yet that's exactly what she'd been wanting: a promise from Wolf that he'd never leave her, couldn't forget her, wouldn't hurt her. But that wasn't realistic or fair. Love didn't make one impervious, but it did help with the bumps and bruises meted out by fate.

Alexandra also knew it was time to silence that insecure voice inside her head, the one that moved in with her when she'd relocated to L.A. Because that frightened, insecure voice was wrong. Beautiful women with great bodies were not more valuable than smart women with kind hearts. The outsides didn't matter more than the insides, and maybe she'd finally believe that Wolf loved her if she learned to love and accept herself.

She owed Wolf an apology. Hoped he'd forgive her and

hoped he still loved her enough to give them and their marriage one more shot.

Pocketing her car keys, Alexandra stepped from the car and took a deep breath for courage. Time to fix this. Time to make things right.

As the car door shut behind her, she heard a crash in the barn. The loud crash was followed by a hollow thud and then a metallic-sounding bang.

What in God's name was that?

She glanced around, searching for signs of life. But the house was dark and, except for the crash and slam sounds coming from the barn, everything was quiet. Too quiet.

Where was everyone? Cormac had said the twins were flying in today, which would mean all five brothers should be here. Where were they? Where was even one?

And for that matter, where was Wolf?

And then, as another thud and bang came from the barn, Alexandra's skin prickled with that sick sixth sense that told her all her questions would be answered once she reached the barn.

Before she'd even gotten the barn door open, she knew from the grunts and groans of pain coming from inside that her brothers were fighting. And with a horrific wave of dread she knew exactly whom they were fighting.

The grunts and groans grew considerably louder as she flung the wide red door open.

"What in God's name are you doing?" she shouted, watching even as one of her brothers—Dillon?—took a hard swing at Wolf.

Wolf had turned to look at her and he took the blow to the side of the head.

Alexandra heard the crack of a knuckled fist against her husband's head, and furious tears started to her eyes. "Stop this! Stop it right now. Wolf. Brock. All of you. Stop it."

And miraculously it did stop. Dillon fell back, bits of straw in his black hair, while Wolf swayed, bloodied, in his place. The others simply looked at her, their faces revealing various bumps and bruises.

"How long has this been going on?" she demanded, entering the barn to circle her brothers before ending in front of Wolf. "Hours?"

"Not hours," Brock answered roughly, the corner of his mouth split and speckled with dried blood. "Maybe an hour." He paused, touched his tongue to his cracked lip. "Maybe two."

She couldn't even look at Wolf. She could already see he'd taken the brunt of the beating. "How? Why?"

Dillon dragged a hand through his hair, knocking the bits of straw out. "It was his idea," he said, nodding at Wolf. "He said he'd fight us—"

"No," Cormac interrupted, glancing down at his right hand and gingerly flexing his fingers into a tender fist. "You were the one that said Wolf had to fight each of us to talk to Alexandra."

"What?" she croaked, taking a step closer to Wolf and staring aghast at her brothers. "You all fought him?" They didn't answer and that was answer enough. She shook her head in disbelief. "Five against one? For one, maybe two hours?"

"It wasn't quite like that," Trey said, grimacing at her description. "We took turns."

"You took turns?" she whispered, livid beyond measure. Her brothers were fighters, she knew that. Nearly every one had been kicked out of school at one point for roughhousing. But they weren't kids anymore, they were men. *Men.* And they'd spent the last hour or so beating up her husband while their father lay in the hospital in an oxygen tent. "If Dad knew what you're doing…" Her voice faded and she looked at them again. "My God, you're all out of your minds."

Dillon made a face. "We did it for you, Alex—"

"Get out!" she snapped, pointing to the barn door. "Get out before I beat each of you—and I won't use my fist, I'll use a shovel or a pitchfork!"

Her brothers quickly trooped out and Alexandra slowly turned to face Wolf, who had a black eye, a bloody nose, swollen lip, bruised cheekbone and a big ugly mark at his temple.

"What were you thinking?" she whispered.

Wolf shrugged wearily. "I wanted to be with you," he said,

swaying on his feet. "I wanted to be here—" he drew a breath and reached up to wipe away blood trickling from a cut in his cheekbone "—for you."

"For me?"

He wiped the blood on the back of his jeans. "You must be worried sick about your dad. If it were my dad, I would be."

"And that's why you're here?"

"Alexandra, I said I'd be there for you anytime you needed me. And so I'm here."

She blinked back tears. He looked as if he'd been run over by a truck. "Getting ambushed by my brothers."

"I was doing okay."

Her lips pursed. "Let's get you to the kitchen and get some ice on those bumps and bruises."

In the kitchen, she directed Wolf to a chair at the scarred pine farm table while she made him an ice pack out of a plastic bag and some ice cubes inside a clean dish towel.

She studied him, ice pack in hand. Blood continued to trickle from a cut in his cheekbone—he might need stitches for that one—and more blood dried at the corner of his lip. His forehead was shadowed with pink and purple. His hair was long, definitely not combed. He hadn't shaved in God knew how long and circles were etched deeply beneath his famous smoldering eyes.

"Wolf, I'm worried some of these cuts will end up in scars."

"I don't care."

"*I* do," she said, pressing the ice pack to his temple, furious all over again.

"Alexandra, I'd fight a hundred men for you. I'd slay dragons, too."

She saw him wince as she shifted the ice pack around on his head. "Wolf, when I said fight for me, I didn't mean literally."

His laugh was low and self-mocking. "I might be too old to box professionally, but I wasn't going to lose you, Alexandra. You're mine. You've been mine from the very beginning."

"When you called me 'ordinary'?" she replied.

He reached up to wrap his hand around her wrist as she held the ice to his temple. "Ordinary's a good thing, love. After ten years of Hollywood nonsense, I welcomed you like a breath of fresh air. It didn't take me long to realize that I might be far from home but you were exactly what I needed. Wanted. Loved."

Alexandra's hand trembled as she clutched the ice pack. Wolf was her undoing. "I don't stand a chance against you, do I?" she murmured.

He tipped his head back, smiled up at her, dark eyes hot, wicked. "No."

And he just kept on melting her heart.

It wasn't fair. She couldn't resist him. And God knew she'd tried.

Wolf's hand warmed hers, and once her trembling stopped, he pulled her hand away, discarded the ice pack and drew her down onto his lap. "Come home, lady," he said, dropping his head to kiss her throat. "Come home with me. Start a family with me."

She leaned against him as his arms went around her. "You forgive me then?"

"There's nothing to forgive. I'm as much at fault as you. I can see now I didn't handle Joy's illness well. I thought I was doing the right thing, but in retrospect I see I only made the problem worse."

"She's better now?"

Wolf's shoulders lifted. "She was in Arizona in rehab for three months. She swears she's done drinking, but it's not my battle anymore. It's hers. We both know it."

Her forehead furrowed with concern. "You were really worried about her."

"I thought she'd die," he answered simply.

Alexandra twisted on his knee to better see his face. *"Die?"*

"My mom was an alcoholic, too." Wolf rubbed his hand over his jaw, and for a moment a shadow of the old torment was back, darkening his eyes. "That's why my father took me away from her when I was twelve. She died less than a year later—alcohol poisoning—and I've always blamed my father. And myself. I hated that we just left her, didn't help her. I thought we might as well have killed her ourselves."

"That's why you couldn't turn your back on Joy," Alexandra concluded softly.

The corner of his mouth lifted, but he still looked tortured. "Those are those ghosts and demons I mentioned." He let out a half sigh. "But trying to help Joy when she didn't want to give up drinking taught me invaluable lessons. We can't help someone that doesn't want to be helped, and in the end, our first responsibility is to ourselves."

She leaned forward, wrapped her arms around his neck, felt his warm, hard chest crush her breasts. And it was a delicious sensation, familiar as well as exciting. "I love you."

"I should have been there for you more, Alexandra. I should have listened to you better—listened with my heart, not my head."

"But you were."

"No—"

"Yes," she whispered, cutting his protest off with a slow and very tender kiss. "I love you, Wolf," she said against his mouth. "I love you more than you'll ever know. I'm just so grateful you're here and that you waited for me and fought for me and didn't give up on me."

He made a rough sound in the back of his throat and stroked her hair back from her face and then along her cheek. "I will always fight for you."

"Even when I get scared and do foolish things?"

"Especially then," he answered soberly.

Alexandra dashed away fresh tears. "I've learned lessons, too. And I know now why I didn't feel loved enough. It wasn't anything you were doing. It was me. I didn't love me enough to believe that you could love me, too."

"How could anyone not love you, Alexandra? Your family dotes on you. Your brothers would go to the ends of the earth for you. And I know this—I will never love anyone the way I love you. I couldn't. You were made for me and I've spent years traveling the world to find you."

Swallowing a soft cry, she dragged her hands through Wolf's

hair, fingers twining in the black, inky length. "So that's how an Irish Spaniard ends up in Los Angeles."

"I came to find my heart."

She blinked even as a tear trickled down her cheek. "I promise you'll never have to search for it again."

Wolf cupped her wet face in his hands. "And I'm going to hold you to that promise," he said roughly before kissing her absolutely senseless.

And maybe, Alexandra thought hours later as she lay snuggled in her husband's strong arms in her rather small child-hood bed, those Hollywood happy endings really do come true.

If you enjoyed what you just read,
then we've got an offer you can't resist!

Take 2 bestselling love stories FREE!

Plus get a FREE surprise gift!

HARLEQUIN *Presents*

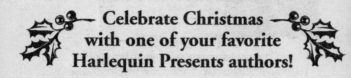

Celebrate Christmas
with one of your favorite
Harlequin Presents authors!

THE SICILIAN'S CHRISTMAS BRIDE

by Sandra Marton

On sale November 2006.

When Maya Sommers becomes Dante Russo's
mistress, rules are made. Although their affair
will be highly satisfying in the bedroom,
there'll be no commitment or future plans.
Then Maya discovers she's pregnant....

Get your copy today!

HARLEQUIN *Presents*

GREEK TYCOONS

They're the men who have everything—except brides...

Wealth, power, charm—what else could a heart-stoppingly handsome tycoon need? In the GREEK TYCOONS miniseries you have already been introduced to some gorgeous Greek multimillionaires who are in need of wives.

Now it's the turn of favorite Presents author

Lynne Graham,

with her attention-grabbing romance...

RELUCTANT MISTRESS, BLACKMAILED WIFE

On sale November 2006.

This tycoon has met his match, and he's decided he has to have her...whatever it takes!